THE BYSTANDER EFFECT

a novel

KRISTIN HELLING

THE BYSTANDER EFFECT
by Kristin Helling

Printed in the United States of America
First Printing, 2017
ISBN 978-1-946921-91-8

Adrenaline
An imprint of Wordwraith Books, LLC

705-B SE Melody Lane #149
Lee's Summit, MO 64063

e-mail wordwraiths@gmail.com
website www.wordwraiths.com
Twitter @Wordwraiths

Edited by Ellen Campbell
Proofread by J. R. Frontera
Cover Design by Austin Helling
Format Design by Kevin G. Summers
Kristin's email author@kristinhelling.com
Kristin's website kristinhelling.com

The Library of Congress Cataloging-in-Publication Data
is available upon request.

For my Husband

Who has always refused to be *just* the bystander in times of need: in the ocean, on the side of the highway, and at the stadium.

"The world will not be destroyed by those who do evil, but by those who stand by and do nothing."

Albert Einstein

TABLE OF CONTENTS

One: Vinnie 1

Two: Raine 7

Three: Vinnie... 15

Four: Detective Heely 19

Five: Raine 29

Six: Detective Heely 35

Seven: Vinnie 41

Eight: Raine 47

Nine: Detective Heely...................................... 53

Ten: Vinnie 57

Eleven: Raine 67

Twelve: Detective Heely.................................... 83

Thirteen: Vinnie 87

Fourteen: Raine 91

Fifteen: Detective Heely 107

Sixteen: Vinnie... 115

Seventeen: Raine.. 121

Eighteen: Detective Heely 129

Nineteen: Raine.. 133

Twenty: Vinnie.. 143

Twenty-One: Detective Heely 149

Twenty-Two: Raine 157

Twenty-Three: Raine....................................... 161

Twenty-Four: Raine... 167

About The Author 174

ONE

Vinnie

Vinnie shifted in the driver's seat as he watched his prey cross the road under the pool of light from a streetlamp. The young brunette tucked her chin while the wind whipped her jacket around her body. The corner of his eye twitched. He leaned over the steering wheel and studied her every step. Her long, bare legs.

She's confident. Comfortable. Enough to take her smart phone out and hold it up to her face.

When she rounded the corner, he scrambled out of the car and eased the door shut, making just the slightest click. Smoothing his greasy hair behind his larger than average ears, he squeezed his eyes shut, then blinked rapidly several times. It was a trick he taught himself to get rid of that annoying twitch.

He looked both ways and crossed the road, pulling the hood of his black jacket over his head.

She stopped in front of an apartment building and poked at her phone. The perfect opportunity. The fawn distracted, unaware of her surroundings. The perfect target, the perfect prey.

He emerged from the shadows behind her, his thoughts turning and shifting like a kaleidoscope. Somehow the handle of the blade found its way into the palm of his sweaty hand. He lunged, and the knife pierced the left side of her back.

She shrieked. Her phone tumbled from palm to pavement. It bounced and flipped over, revealing the shattered screen.

It happened in a blur. She tried to turn, but he caught her throat with his forearm and yanked out his knife. Another scream. He plunged it into her fleshy lower back. Again.

She staggered and doubled over but recovered, using the door to brace herself.

The keys she fumbled in her hand caught his attention. She must have pulled them from her pocket.

Vinnie spotted the pepper spray on the keychain and almost laughed. Pepper spray. Pathetic.

A voice cut across the sound of her panic: the whimpers, the hitching breaths and choked cries. It was a man. Vinnie craned his neck and saw the man leaning out of a window from the apartment complex across the street.

"Hey! You!"

He yanked out the blade, now dripping dark, syrupy liquid and ran, almost tripping over his own feet. Rounding the corner and cowering in the alley, he held the knife so it dripped on the cement. He didn't like messy. Blood on his clothing. He regretted his weapon every time. But he always went back to the knife. It was as if he forgot until after the task was finished. Plus, a knife was the easiest thing to get his hands on at home.

A blade required close proximity to the victim. It was quiet, apart from the screaming of course. It brought him a certain release that his mind craved deeply. And the urge ripped him from the inside out. The only way to make it stop was to fulfill the need.

He looked back around the corner to see that the man who'd been shouting had slammed his window shut.

No doubt he thought it was some sort of lover's quarrel. A common occurrence in the city. Nothing to bat an eye at.

But the girl was getting away.

He waited there a moment longer listening for sirens, but nothing came. He peeked again and saw the shattered phone in a pool of blood. The girl had no personal lifeline anymore. The door to the apartment building stood ajar.

He hunched his scrawny frame and crept from the alley, crushing the cell phone under his boot. Using his sleeve, he pushed open the door. If there was one thing he was good at, it was paying attention to detail. Making no mistakes, leaving no tracks.

She'd made it to the elevator. She lay in a heap on the ground, her bare legs tangled under her. Vinnie kept his hood up as he perused her. Deep crimson stained her body and marred the floor behind her. He was sure the first stab wounds were fatal, but they weren't enough to satisfy his need. Using his boot, he pushed her body onto its back, facing him.

Tears still streamed down her cheeks, leaving streaks of black from her makeup. Eyelids half closed, she stared into his face, biting her lip. "Why?" she croaked.

That was a question he could not answer.

He smelled the liquor on her breath.

It was taking too long to kill her.

His hand acted as if of its own volition, raising the knife. She kicked at him and he stabbed once more. She tried to scramble back, but he caught her knees and forced them apart. He heard shouting, slurred words that sounded like a mixture of 'help' and refusals.

"Why are you doing this to me?" she sobbed.

"Because I felt like killing a woman tonight." The air was stark. Thin. Cold. The blade was slippery in his hand. He stabbed her one last time in the chest, the blow that ripped her life up through the knife and into him.

Vinnie rifled her clothing and found her keys, and pocketed them. Having the keys would make his job much easier later. He stood up and stared at the scene, then turned and left the apartment lobby. He ran to the alley and stripped off his black jacket smothered in blood. He threw it into the dumpster, and took off down the road to his car, the knife still in hand.

Vinnie closed the door to the garage of his suburban home and went directly to a small shower pan and faucet he'd installed for washing up after yard work. He stripped and sprayed all the sweat off him. The handheld sprayer trembled in his hands.

What did I do? So much blood. Deep crimson swirled over the drain. He cleaned the knife, and then stepped out.

I had to do it. The urges. The humiliation. He dried himself with a towel and dressed in the boxer briefs he'd left on the workbench. He rolled up the bloodied clothes and stuffed them deep in a bag of lawn debris. He looked down at himself, his chest rising and falling with his shallow breaths.

Was that enough? Did I leave any traces? It was sloppy and uncalculated. He'd need to up his game…

Inside, the wood floor was cold on his bare feet. Tiptoeing down the hall, he was careful to avoid every creaky spot in the old house. He turned the knob of a door on the right. Moonlight streamed through the window, bathing the crib. He reached in and placed his hand on the baby girl's fuzzy head. The energy went through the hand, up his arms and into his chest. The trembling numbness in his fingers and hands dissipated. He turned from the crib and crossed the hall into the bedroom opposite.

He crept around the bed, and scanned the body of the woman there. She had the quilt pulled over her face.

"How's Scarlett?" she groaned from under the comforter.

"Huh?" he asked, jumping out of his skin at the sound of her voice. *She's not sleeping yet?*

"The baby?" She turned over and looked at him with bleary eyes.

"Oh... yeah... She's great. Sleeping like a baby." He flashed a quick smile before crawling into the cool sheets. He shivered as he pulled up the covers. His wife made an indistinct '*mmm*' and rolled over.

Vinnie lay there until he heard her breathing slow. She was finally asleep. She must have been vaguely aware he'd left the room. She didn't realize how long he'd been gone and must have thought he'd only gotten up to check on the baby.

She didn't smell San Francisco's night air on him.

She didn't smell the murder.

TWO

Raine

Raine Walsh placed a palm on her abs as she bounced on the bright blue Pilates ball at her desk. She peered at the glowing computer screen and then back to the paperwork that sat in front of her. Concentration broke at the sound of the deep bark, which made her heart jump into her throat.

She looked at the sandy pit bull mix across the room.

"Viona, what did I say about making noise? You won't be able to come here if you bark! You gotta go outside again?" She stood and fished her foot around under the desk for her black ballet flats. The dog's tail wiggled the back half of her body back and forth.

"All right, all right." She clicked her tongue for Viona to follow as she headed for the door. She opened her office door and assessed the waiting room. There was a married couple on the sofa, as well as a man in his early twenties in the corner armchair.

The receptionist looked up from her makeshift desk, fashioned out of a dining room table. "Again?" she laughed, as Viona bobbed back and forth behind Raine's legs. "You want me to take her this time?"

"Naw, it's okay. Thanks, Sylvie." Raine smiled. "Vee, c'mon," she called and turned left down the hall to the back door. She leaned in the doorway and watched her dog smell every blade of grass in the small yard behind the house.

Raine loved the house-turned-office. Though it had been a tough decision, she and Marcus decided not to move their practice, despite everything they'd been through last year. Both of them had patients that counted on them. They had clients every day that were dealing with their own nightmares, and needed continuity. They both agreed that if they moved, it would throw away the foundation they'd built in their still-young practice.

And even though time had passed, Raine was still picking up the pieces of her life to puzzle them back together. She had struggled with even stepping foot in this building again after the murder of Troy Batterman, their partner in the practice. She still saw vivid images every time she tried to sleep. Or when she looked at his office, the room across from hers, right next to Marcus's.

But as much as it brought back memories, it was also a huge relief. Towards the end, Troy's behavior in the office caused her unnecessary stress and anxiety. At one point she'd even thought he had something to do with her abduction last year.

Apart from their feelings, there was also a question of whether they could legally continue their practice there, since Troy owned the building. During the time Raine recovered in the hospital, Marcus began looking for another practice to join.

They carried on with funeral services, and when Troy's will was being executed, a lawyer contacted Marcus. In the event of an untimely death—which had been the case—Troy left the house to Marcus. It worked out.

Of course there was the matter of Troy's clients. Neither Raine nor Marcus handled the type of cases Troy specialized in, so they referred his clients to other psychologists in the area.

Raine clapped her hands together to call Viona, who had continued to sniff every tree, shrub, and flower around the building. The pit mix ran back in with her tail between her legs, and galloped into the waiting room.

"Vee!" she shouted as she followed her in. Viona was currently licking the neck and face of the man that had been sitting in the armchair.

"I apologize." She laughed, her cheeks hot as she grabbed Viona's collar and led the dog back to her office. "She's bored."

Marcus stepped out of his office and left the door cracked. He smiled at Raine, and picked up a chart from Sylvie's desk. "Hey there, Rob. You ready to head back?"

The guy stood and wiped his face with the back of his sleeve. "I don't mind her. She's sweet."

She nodded at Marcus as he took his client back to his office.

Sylvie smiled. "I think it's great having her around the office, Dr. Walsh. She's a calming spirit. It's good therapy."

Raine nodded and closed the door behind her. Viona *was* good therapy, not just for their clients, but for Raine as well. *I think Sylvie knows that,* she thought. She crouched to pour water into Viona's bowl from a reusable bottle.

She situated herself back on the Pilates ball behind her desk. She woke up the computer screen and checked the paper files. It was back to work.

Since she'd returned, 'back to work' meant transferring her client's files into the computer—converting her handwritten notes to digital. The thought crossed her mind that if she was unable to continue with a client's therapy, and she needed to transfer their files to an affiliated therapist, it'd be easier in digital form.

Worst case scenario, of course.

Viona had finally settled down at her feet. The consistent motion of the dog's breathing was soothing. It allowed her to chip away at the tedious work in front of her.

Later, when she checked the time on the clock at the bottom of the computer screen, she saw that several hours had passed. It was nearing the end of her workday. In recent days, Raine would not stay at the office after hours alone. She rented the yoga therapy room out to a few other instructors she knew that could use the space. She didn't want to put herself in the position of being alone in her office again. It wasn't safe.

She was working through this with her own therapist. Finding situations that made her feel safe. Trying to free herself from feeling confined by that cage in that prison, or the boundaries she set for herself in her mind.

The knock on her door made her jump.

"Yes?" she called out.

Sylvie peeked her head in. "There's a gentleman here to see you."

"I don't have any appointments."

Sylvie cleared her throat. "It's a police officer."

Raine stood up, Viona mirroring her actions. She kicked the Pilates ball under the desk and made her way around. "Can you please take Vi out for a bit, Sylvie? Thank you."

"Of course!" She pushed open the door and patted Viona on the head.

Raine leaned over and grabbed the neglected leash off her desk. She handed it over to Sylvie with a smile, though her nervousness was beginning to build. A police officer visiting could mean many things, good or bad.

On the one hand, they could come bearing news of information they discovered about her case. The bad guy had gotten away. The Warden was never found. She'd spent too long in the hospital unconscious after they rescued her, and the Warden was able to pack up shop and skip town, along with the rest of the innocent victims she'd spent time with in the simulated prison facility. He'd even stripped the skyscraper penthouse down to its walls, leaving no traces. The only ounce of evidence they had in their possession—besides Raine and Arie getting away—was the fact that they had the Warden's secret accomplice, Megan, locked up in a state prison facility. Any and all information would be good. On the other hand there could also be bad news. Maybe the innocent people she couldn't save when she managed to escape were dead. These were all possibilities.

"Go right in," Sylvie said as the man approached her office.

Her stomach plunged and flipped when she recognized his face. It was a cop she'd seen before.

It was the same clean-shaven, blond haired policeman that was there when she woke up in the hospital. The first authority figure—other than her nurse—that she'd spoken to. Memories of the hospital came flooding back to her, and she felt like she needed to steady herself.

"Hello, Raine." He smiled politely at her, extending his hand. "I heard your receptionist say I was a cop?" He pulled out his identification and held it out. "I was. I'm a detective now. You're looking good. It's good to see you again. Much better circumstances than the last."

Raine stared at him, wide-eyed. "You found him?" she whispered.

He dropped his gaze, and shook his head. "No, I'm sorry." It appeared as though he was struggling to find the right words. As if he hadn't prepared them before he came to her. "That's not why I'm here."

She brushed the thought from her mind, regaining her professional demeanor. The emotion smoothed from her face, and she looked over her shoulder at the burning lavender incense. "I'm so sorry. How rude of me. Please come in, have a seat." She guided him to the sitting area. She chose the sofa instead of her usual armchair. This wasn't a session. The armchair didn't feel right.

"I prefer to stand." When he saw her dismay, he quickly changed his mind." Actually, I think I will sit. I've been on my feet all day. Thank you." He sat across from her on the edge of the armchair. "Do you remember me?"

"Of course. Though I don't remember your name. Sorry about that."

He stifled a laugh. "No, It's my fault. I'm Jonah Heely. Please call me Jonah."

Yeah, she didn't remember that name at all. She folded her hands in her lap and leaned forward on the couch.

"I've come to you for your professional guidance."

She shuffled on the couch. "Oh—I'm not... I'm currently not taking new clients. I'm sure Marcus will be able to oblige—"

Jonah chuckled. "No, I'm not asking you to be my therapist."

"Is that funny?" She brushed an errant lock of hair away, making the crease between her eyes evident. She loosened her jaw. She'd been clenching it since he walked in.

His expression was immediately serious again. "I'm sorry. What I mean is, I'm working on another case. And I'm having trouble with it. With everything I uncover, I can't get *you* out of my head. By that, I mean, because of your horrific experience last year, and with your professional training and education, I think you could really help us out. I wasn't sure who else to turn to."

Raine sat back on the couch, soaking in the information that Jonah was telling her. "Why would my experience help?" she asked, her voice barely audible.

"What happened to you has some striking similarities to this case. I can't give you many of the details right now. I'd have to have you come down to the station and sign

NDAs before I can discuss the case with you, that is, if you agree to help."

She still didn't see how she could help them. If they needed her experience as a psychologist, well, she was still trying to get back in the groove. But maybe doing something like this would help her get back into it. Maybe it would get her out of this office where memories drifted into the room from the empty office across the hall. It could help her get her life back. More importantly, maybe she *could* provide something that would actually help with the case and the victims involved.

"You can take some time and think about it," he added. "I know it's not an easy decision to work with law enforcement, of any kind. But I didn't know where else to turn. And I'm glad to see you're doing well here."

She nodded.

They stood at the same time.

Jonah moved towards the door.

Raine stood in front of the couch.

"There's one more thing, though I didn't want to tell you until right before I left, because I knew it would distract you, and I needed your attention for just those few minutes."

She raised an eyebrow, her stomach giving another sickly flutter.

"She's talking."

Raine felt the energy wash over her as if it cracked over her skull like an egg. He could only be talking about one person. The only person who hadn't spoken since she was locked up.

Megan.

THREE

Vinnie

It was far too soon for the alarm to be going off. After smacking the snooze, Vinnie laid there in a fog for a few more minutes. He stretched out over the empty mattress. His wife was already up for the day. He craned his neck to see the time. 7:30am. He squeezed his eyes shut. It had been a late night last night. But this morning he felt exhilarated, as if a heavy weight had been lifted off his chest. He was light. No, he was free.

But the feeling was fleeting. It always was. He kicked off the blankets and rolled over, wondering if he could stay in bed. Then the nutty aromatic coffee filled his nose.

"Wanna cup?"

He jerked his head up. Gwen was standing in the doorway, the sun making her long, blond hair glow. She wore an oversized button up nightshirt and her legs were bare.

"Yes," he breathed, grateful for the wife, who'd already gotten up, fed the baby, and made the coffee. He stood up and joined her, took the mug from her hands, and drove it to his lips. Before it reached his mouth, he felt the steam on his face. He sipped to avoid burning himself. The smell was enough to shake off the grogginess.

He followed Gwen to the family room. She continued past the island that separated the rooms, and into the kitchen.

In the family room Vinnie bent down to kiss Scarlett on the head as she sat in her swing. He shook his head at the program Gwen had on the TV. She called out from behind the refrigerator door, "Hey you know that girl they found in the dumpster? They're saying they still haven't found the guy that took her yet. Gonna do a 20/20 on it in a few weeks."

"Babe, why do you watch this garbage?" He picked up the remote and flipped the channel.

She stifled a laugh as dishes clanked in the sink. "The news?"

"Yeah, it's all depressing." And dangerous. He definitely did not want his little adventure last night becoming a prime topic for Gwen. It was a done deal.

"I'll tell you what's depressing."

He looked up to see her pointing at the opened mail on the kitchen island.

The draft on the back of his bare shoulders was chilly. He should have put a shirt on before coming out here, though he'd be getting dressed for work soon anyway.

The papers were spread out on the counter. He set down his coffee cup down and picked up the closest one. Electric bill. He let it drop back to the counter. He made sure his wife's back was to him while he shuffled through the rest. Mortgage. Water bill. Cell phones. The words on the papers blurred in his vision. Red marks announcing PAST DUE flashed at him. Closing in on him. Trapping him. Restricting. He dropped them back to the counter, his hands balling into fists.

She looked over her shoulder at him. "It'll be okay. You get a check next week, yeah? And I'm getting another shipment of product soon."

Gwen wanted to be a representative for a company that sold comfortable clothes to women. It was great and all, a nice distraction for her while she stayed home all day, but he didn't like that the representatives had to buy everything up front, and then turn around and sell it. That was money going out, and none coming in. At least not very quickly. But it made her happy.

She swiveled around, pushed the bills aside and leaned toward him.

He bent in for a kiss. He loved that her bottom lip was so much fuller than her thin upper lip.

"We could sell the baby." He tried to smile and looked over his shoulder at Scarlett, drooling impressively as she kicked her pudgy legs in the swing.

Gwen laughed and swatted at his shoulder before she turned back to the sink.

"I gotta go to work," he mumbled, sliding easily back into the depression that always heralded another day at the office.

Vinnie pushed open the door. Mud tracked in on people's shoes smeared the pasty green linoleum floor. The whole department of motor vehicles had a stained and shabby feel. He had to veer left by the humming coke machines to avoid being funneled into one of the lines. The signs were stark: car registration and title, driver's license renewal, and so on.

A beefy man holding the small slip of paper with his number on it glared at Vinnie for trying to cut in the line.

Vinnie looked at his feet and kept going to a door that led to the back. He punched his clock-in number and put his lunch bag—a crinkled up brown bag saturated with grease stains—into the fridge. He'd be lucky if it was still there later.

"Vin. We need you in lane four."

Red. Blood. Flashes of the night before.

He snapped his head up to see a coworker, the one with the *red* curls and cat's eye glasses staring at him.

"All right, I just got here so lemme—"

"Now."

He pursed his lips and slammed the refrigerator door. Typical. They couldn't keep up and needed to throw the next shift to the wolves to pick up their slack. He rubbed at his eye, the one with the twitch, and made his way to the front desk.

Things in his station had been moved around. He huffed as he put the post-it notes back on the left side. He turned the computer monitor to the exact angle he'd had it before.

Why are people moving my shit? He cringed when he felt a breath on the back of his neck. He shot a glance over his shoulder and didn't see anybody there. He yanked back the "next window please" sign, then looked up at the angry faces of the customers in line.

He slapped the button that displayed the next number in line.

Only eight hours of turning people down for not having the correct paperwork, and being spit at for charging a fee for using credit cards to pay. Only eight more hours.

FOUR

Detective Heely

J onah pressed the gas pedal as the light turned green, easing into acceleration. He reached up and scratched under his nose, still surprised that Raine Walsh was sitting in his passenger seat. He never imagined that she'd agree to work with him on this case. Or the fact that she agreed to be picked up at her apartment in his unimpressive unmarked car. The Criminal Investigations Division avoided the standard patrol car model so he wouldn't get pegged as law enforcement.

His whole life changed when Raine came into it, first at the hospital after they recovered her body from the landfill where the dump truck dropped her. Her case was something that he thought about every single night before he closed his eyes. He'd spent every waking hour trying to understand every possible nuance of the information from eyewitness accounts, and unearth a lead to the man who did this to her.

Of course they had Megan. But was she a win? She was an accomplice. But she was being difficult. She'd always been difficult. A closed book. The first time he'd seen any trace of emotion on the girl's face was when he brought her parents in. But she caught herself and withdrew again.

Some terrible brainwashing must have happened to her after her disappearance.

The parents.

They couldn't understand why their daughter—kidnapped from them years ago—was behind bars. Of course Jonah, along with many other people in authority, had explained to them that she'd assumed a new identity in a different city. That she'd stolen drugs from her place of employment, among other felonies, and attempted homicide.

And without Megan's co-operation, there had been no other leads on the case. Where was the perpetrator, the one the victim witnesses called the Warden? Where were the other victims Raine claimed to be with? Quite frankly, he'd gone back and forth several times on whether any of this even happened. He didn't believe any of it until Arie came forward and corroborated the wild story. But if the two of them fabricated it, they were playing a good game.. The fact that Megan was in the picture made things more plausible.

It killed him that this case was slipping from him. The more time between leads—if he got any lead—the harder it would be. It could end up in the cold case files. He'd never had a case like this, in all the years he'd been in law enforcement.

"It feels weird sitting in this car. I know I'm in the passenger seat, but riding in a cop car is unnerving, even though it doesn't look like one."

Her voice pulled him out of his thoughts, though he didn't show it on the outside. "Why's that?"

"I feel like I'm in trouble, like I've done something wrong." She turned her head away from him, towards the passenger window.

"Have you? Done something wrong?"

"No."

"Then why do you feel that way? Honestly, Raine. You're a colleague." He extended the compliment and hoped she'd take it, hoping he hadn't pushed too far.

"It's the same feeling I had in the cage, when I convinced myself that I'd done something to get myself locked up there. That I'd done something terrible, even if I couldn't remember it. I see it all the time with clients. People always try to understand. They need to be able to explain things to themselves. And they block out negative events and information as a coping mechanism."

"He was a monster. You didn't do anything to deserve that." The radio interrupted them with a squelch followed by unintelligible—to Raine—voices. He listened carefully to the different codes and acronyms, and then tuned it out.

"You know I'm doing everything in my power to generate leads on your case. I haven't stopped."

"I appreciate that." She folded her hands in her lap. "I haven't either."

Jonah stifled a laugh, but not because what she said was funny. He hoped she wasn't going out and digging into dangerous things on her own. He needed to ask her to make sure that was not the case. She was apparently still struggling with what had happened. Perhaps he'd ask her later, but not now. Not the right time or place.

He turned the car at the precinct and parked in his usual spot. "So, I just need you to sign a few papers and we'll get right to it, okay?" he asked as they headed for the building. He looked back at Raine, who nodded. He opened the door and held it for her. "Just to your left there." He nodded at Maxine, the secretary behind the desk.

His office was to the left. Nothing special. He wondered in passing what Raine thought of his converted closet office. He didn't even have windows. The place looked like he spent little to no time there. Or little to no time organizing it anyway. There were papers everywhere. If he'd known Raine would agree so quickly, he would have at least cleaned up the three-ring binders mixed with manila folders piled on his desk. He made a mental note to organize them in the filing cabinet later, which probably wouldn't happen. His boss would be asking for the digital reports soon. He needed to file them in the records management system on his computer, but it was such a pain in the ass. He preferred the physical stuff.

He drew keys from the retractable clip on his belt, unlocked the desk, and grabbed his steno pad of notes.

"Looks like you need to do what I've been doing." Raine laughed as she looked around. "I've been transcribing all my client notes into the computer system. We just got a new system and well, Marcus thinks it'd be more organized if their files were all in one digital location."

He motioned for her to sit in the seat across from him.

She took his cue.

"Marcus? Is that the guy who was with you in the hospital?"

She nodded.

"Are you two still seeing each other?" he asked. "Ah, never mind. It's none of my business." He let out an airy laugh and pulled back to a page on his notebook.

"It's okay. We are. We actually moved in together."

"Oh, right. He was a nice guy." He spun in the chair and grabbed a manila folder from the cabinet behind him. He laid it out in front of her. "Read this and sign on the bottom of the second page. We need an NDA on file since this is an ongoing case. Strictly confidential. No speaking to media. No withholding any information you may know."

"Right," she said, scanning over the paperwork.

He watched her flip the sheet over and scribble her name at the bottom.

"When will I get to speak with Megan?" she asked.

It surprised him she hadn't asked sooner. "I was expecting you to ask that."

"I figured if I helped you, you'd help me."

He nodded. This was something that had already occurred to him. His boss wasn't too keen on letting a victim speak with the perpetrator, but sometimes in cases like this one, it was actually beneficial—potentially extracting more emotion or information from the accused. With Raine's professional background, it made the decision easier.

"We've called Arie in. We're waiting for him to get there." He watched her pull back in the chair. Had she forgotten about him? Or was the mention of his name a gentle reminder that there were others involved as well?

He continued, "So, the case at hand. We found a vehicle off the road. Abandoned there with the keys in the ignition. What caught our attention was that it was engulfed in flames."

Raine gasped.

"The scene was just too familiar. I immediately thought about your case—as if I'm not thinking about it all the time anyway," he finished.

"The Warden."

"See, that's originally what we thought. Car abandoned, the registered owner of the vehicle is a girl in her twenties and missing. But then..." he grabbed his water bottle, downing a mouthful before continuing, "...we found the victim. The body of a young woman was found in the lobby of her apartment building when neighbors started leaving for work in the morning. So, I stopped wondering if this was connected to your case.

"So then why do we need you? It's clear that your kidnapping was different—that this may be an isolated incident. The Warden doesn't kill on the spot. He's a serial kidnapper. He holds his victims. The scary thing here, and the reason we brought you in, is because this case... this case is eerily similar to another one. Not yours in particular, but the fact is, this modern case was nearly a identical to a case that is in the archives. Just like your case had parallels to the Stanford Prison Experiment. We believe this one is patterned on the case of Kitty Genovese in 1964. The very case that sparked the 3-digit emergency code that we still use today, 911."

"This girl was killed in the lobby of her apartment building? Surely people must have heard her. But no one helped?" Her expression was pained.

Jonah was almost certain Raine had studied the Kitty Genovese case. After all, she had her PhD in psychology.

"For the same reason they didn't help Kitty in the sixties. The phrase, 'The Bystander Effect' was coined during this case. This killer isn't stupid. He knows what he's doing. And he's using this psychological phenomenon to his advantage."

"So he uses the bystander effect to his advantage and kills in broad daylight?" she asked.

"We don't have enough evidence to prove that. I'm only going by the little information we have so far. But with your background, I thought you could be of help. Maybe help us get into this person's mind a little better."

"Well, you're not giving me much to go on."

Jonah stretched his arms over his head.

"I'm sure you're doing your due diligence. I believe that. All I'm saying is, you have one victim. What if it's co-incidence that he happened to do it in the apartment lobby? How can you be sure it's a copycat?"

"There is... more than one victim." He should have told her sooner. But the Kitty Genovese case was fresher in his mind, so he started there. "A man was found stabbed to death at his place of employment. It was a construction site. I'm talking heavy equipment and girders. In broad daylight. We've questioned his coworkers; some of them claimed they'd just taken a break with him not long before he was found. There were a lot of people in the vicinity."

"How do you know they're connected?"

"The same murder weapon was used in both cases, according to the Medical Examiner."

Raine nodded. "How does it prove your copycat theory?"

Boy, she was full of questions. He liked it. It was exactly the perspective he needed on the case. Going to Raine was the perfect decision: he needed fresh eyes, and she needed a distraction. He hoped it wasn't too overwhelming for her.

"The killer uses the public to his advantage. He's doing his killings right in plain sight, but nobody seems to see him. There's no description of this guy. In both cases, I'm sure people saw him, but they can't give an accurate depiction of what they saw."

"Surveillance at all? I mean, an apartment building. A construction site. Surely there are cameras somewhere?"

"None that covered the scenes. I'm sure the perpetrator checked that out as well."

Someone knocked.

"Heely, a Mr. Webb is here to see you," Maxine announced.

The thin, ashen-haired boy entered the office.

Raine leapt from her seat and embraced him.

Jonah thought he saw her whisper something into his ear. Maybe they had stayed in contact.

"Don't get comfortable, guys. Since Arie is here now—" he reached forward and shook Arie's hand, "—we're going to head over to the facility where Megan's being held." He followed them out of his small office, into the lobby. "Why don't you go ahead, and I'll be right there, okay?"

As they started out of the building, he turned back toward his office.

"Are you going with them, Heely?" Maxine asked as the door closed behind Arie and Raine.

His phone vibrated with an incoming call. He slid it out of his pocket and checked the number. "Uhh, yeah, I'll be right there. Give me just a moment."

She nodded.

Jonah accepted the call, and closed the door to his office. "Hey there."

"Hi hon, what are you up to?"

"I'm working, what are you doing?"

"I've just been to the laundromat. Now I'm headed to get some groceries. I wanted to see if you needed anything." The man on the line sounded exasperated, as if he were walking at a brisk pace down the street, most likely carrying the laundry basket.

"I don't think so—except, did you grab that list on the fridge?"

"List?"

"Ben..."

"I'm joking. Chill out, man. I got the list."

Jonah rubbed his eyes with his thumb and index finger, feeling the familiar anxiety pull at him.

"Are you going to be home for dinner tonight, Jonah? I'm making apricot glazed chicken with garlic spinach on the side. We could pop open that bottle of red we got as a housewarming present."

He sighed, being careful not to let his partner hear it. "All of that sounds so great, Ben. But you know how it goes. I'm working a big case right now and we've had some breakthroughs. Dinner sounds wonderful, but I can't make any promises."

Now it was Benjamin's turn to sigh, only he didn't seem to care if Jonah heard. "There's always a big case, Jonah. When does it end? Where does your professional life stop and your personal life begin?"

"I don't need this right now."

"Right. Yeah, okay. I'm at the store now anyway. I'll see you when I see you."

"Ben!" He wanted to catch him before he hung up. "I'll make it up to you okay? I'm not saying I'm completely out for dinner. I'll give you a call closer to, okay?"

There was hesitation on the line. "Kay."

"Hey, I love you. You got that?"

"Yeah, man. Love you too. Later." The phone clicked.

Jonah slipped his phone in his pocket, rubbed his eyes, and sighed again. It was time to get back to work.

FIVE

Raine

"Now remember, Dr. Walsh. Do not allow the convicted criminal to manipulate you."

Raine nodded and smoothed her hand over her hair as he briefed her outside the interrogation room.

Megan hadn't spoken in months. As an inmate she was compliant, but she wouldn't speak. Raine was going to be approaching the visit as a professional, rather than a victim. She was only granted access to Megan because of her credentials. It surprised her they were even allowing that, considering her conflict of interest. The fact that it was *her* case.

"There's no way I will allow the subject to manipulate me." Her face was resolute, but she wasn't entirely sure she believed it. Maybe a year ago she would have, but she'd been manipulated by Megan before. She couldn't and wouldn't let it happen again.

Arie spoke out behind her, "I still don't understand why I can't go in with her."

She offered him a sympathetic look. It hadn't been her decision to go into the room alone.

Detective Heely heaved a sigh. "You're lucky to even be here right now, Arie. I thought it was appropriate for you to be here to support Raine, but it's in your best interest to watch from behind the glass. You may be able to provide some insight as well."

"So if Raine was a victim and only a victim, she wouldn't be allowed in there?"

"No."

Arie exaggerated crossing his arms over his chest.

"Whenever you're ready, they'll bring her in. Arie and I will be right on the other side of this mirror, okay? You just signal and I'll be right in there."

She turned around when the metal door opened. She saw the scene through the one-way glass. She looked at Arie, then turned back to the mirror. A woman officer guided the cuffed red haired girl into the room.

Raine's gut wrenched. Megan was still dainty, but her face had hollowed out since the last time she'd seen her. Her pale face had a sour expression. The cop sat her down in the chair and locked the handcuffs and shackles to the table.

Was that really necessary? Raine steeled herself to go into the room. She looked down at her notebook. She wasn't sure she'd use it, but the comfort of having a pen and paper on hand when she spoke to clients always helped to ease the apprehension. And even though she'd had to get to the bottom of someone's life to find clarity and happiness many times before, this was different. She needed to coax information from Megan. Any kind of information. Any words at all.

She looked back at Arie and Heely once more before she stepped forward.

"Just say the word," Heely reminded her.

As the female officer left, Raine walked into the hall. The officer nodded to her, and then turned to allow her to pass through the door.

Raine put her hand on the knob and pulled the heavy door open and entered the interrogation room. The red haired girl's back was to Raine, and she didn't react when the door slammed.

Raine hesitated then approached. She pulled out the chair with a screech, and sat. Rage and despair threatened to overwhelm her, but she had to control herself, or she'd lose this opportunity. Arie and Jonah were just on the other side of that wall. She needed to keep it together.

She looked at Megan, taking in the deep, dark circles under her eyes. Her hair had dulled. She looked in far worse shape than when they were in the makeshift prison.

Raine had rehearsed everything she wanted to say, but now that she was here, she was floundering. They sat together in silence, for almost too long.

Raine finally spoke. "Three months ago, did you think we'd be here?" She kept her voice even, but the words hung there between them.

Megan glanced up at Raine and looked back down.

"I didn't." She answered her own question. "Can I ask you another question?"

"You're going to ask me why. Why did I do it?" Megan's voice was raspy. She still didn't look up.

Raine raised her eyebrow. *She speaks!* "I don't need to ask that question." She shoved aside her animosity and forced herself to be professional. "I see it all the time. Depressed clients can't give me a reason why they feel depressed. There is no reason. I'm not saying you fall in this category. I think there's a reason you've acted the way you have. And I daresay it wasn't your fault in the beginning. If anything we shared together was true." She thought she saw a flicker of emotion on Megan's face, but it was gone quickly. "Why are you depriving yourself of basic necessities here? What's your end game?"

Megan finally looked up.

Raine kept her face neutral as she stared into Megan's flecked green pupils. Not even a quiver or a twitch. "It's just me and you talking here."

Megan said, "He's not coming back for me."

Raine knew who she meant without having to ask. She decided to go with her instincts.

"Megan." She reached for the girl's hand.

Megan jerked away, a snarl on her lips.

Raine had overplayed it. She silently cursed herself, regretting her instinctive response. She needed to evaluate the needs of *this* person, like she would with any other client.

"You are also a victim here. You've had a psychological response that causes hostages to develop sympathetic sentiments towards their captors. A survival mechanism caused you to share his opinions and develop romantic feelings."

"Have you told any of these people what *you* did with Allen? During your... alone time?"

Raine almost looked back at the mirror but stopped herself. Nothing happened during her alone time except the incessant fear and brainwashing. She'd been lucky to escape rape, even though the fear never left her. She had no idea what happened to her when she was unconscious. He was trying to show her how little control she had in her captivity. That her privacy was gone, and her identity stripped. "I don't know what you think went on. Nothing happened," she stated flatly.

"It had been all about me until you showed up. He started to lose interest in me. I was worried he'd forgotten what we had."

"Megan, how could you be jealous of me? I didn't want that."

"But Allen did."

"He didn't love you. He didn't love me." Her professionalism was slipping. "What about the others in the prison? Think about Arie. He had a connection with you. I thought you were upset because of the time I spent with Arie. He talked about you a lot." Raine's throat constricted. "Did he mean nothing to you?" she asked.

Megan shook her head, her lip trembling.

Raine turned and pointed at the mirror. "He's watching. Behind that mirror. He saw what you just did."

Megan looked down at her lap.

Raine saw the opportunity. "He knows you used him to try and find me. To kill me."

"I always protected him. I didn't want him hurt."

"You protected him by letting him go. But the others, well they weren't so lucky. They're all still missing. What happened to them, Megan? You could turn all this around. You could protect them too."

"No one could protect them." She raised her eyes, but kept her chin down. Then she smirked.

A massive chill slinked up Raine's arms and down her spine. "So this is what you want? You finally start talking and nothing but shit comes out. I'm done here." She pushed her chair back and stood, then marched to the door and knocked twice.

The officer opened the door. Raine went to join Arie, who continued to watch Megan, who sat staring at the table.

Raine's temples began to throb. Exhaustion tugged behind her eyes, though she wouldn't show it.

"She said 'could'," Arie whispered.

"Huh?" Raine was lost.

"She said, 'no one *could* protect them' not, 'no one *can* protect them'. She used the past tense, as if they're already gone. As if we're too late."

Raine froze. He was right. That was exactly what Megan said.

Raine realized that Detective Heely was gone. "Arie, where's Jonah?" she asked.

"He rushed out of here. He got a lead on another case he's working on. Something about finding another victim."

She tensed. "Did you hear anything else, anything at all?"

He didn't take his eyes off Megan. "Yes. The victim is alive."

SIX

Detective Heely

J onah pressed the accelerator and weaved in and out of traffic. As he approached a cross street, the light turned yellow, but he ignored it.

The day had already turned out to be more work than he intended. He didn't have time to deal with the fact that his stomach was protesting missing lunch. For the first time in quite a while, he was making progress on both cases.

The fact that they found a victim alive was fantastic. That survivor, depending what condition they were in, would be able to give them invaluable insight. He'd met Raine in a similar situation.

After he pushed through the doors of the hospital, he flashed his badge at the front desk, and worked his way down the familiar hallway.

A woman wearing scrubs stood between him and the double doors that led to the victim's location. "Sir, you can't come in here."

He had to hand it to them; the hospital enforced their rules every time, no matter what. And the nurses were politer than they needed to be.

"Excuse me, I'm working on a case that involves a man in there."

"That's very nice, sir. I'll allow you to see him, but not yet." The nurse leaned toward him. "He's lost a lot of blood. It's a wonder he's alive. We'll let you know when he's stable and ready to speak to you, but I can tell you it probably won't be today."

"Every minute counts right now." He couldn't hide his exasperation.

"I'm not just being stickler here, Detective. He's under sedation right now, and they're prepping him for surgery. I'm not sure how much information you'd be able to get."

He reached into his pocket and pulled out a business card. "All right. But if he comes to and starts talking, you call me right away."

The nurse looked at the card, but didn't take it. "You can give it to the front desk. We'll be sure to contact you." She nodded and without another word, she turned and went through the double doors.

Jonah wanted to curse, but he spun around and scanned the ER lobby. Glimpses of blood and anxious people. He saw an argument taking place at the front desk. Something about insurance coverage. Across the room, a couple sat together, leaning on each other.

This was not a place he liked to be.

Go home, Jonah, a voice hissed in his mind. After the angry woman left the desk, he walked up to it and slipped his card across the counter. He repeated what he'd told the nurse.

He returned to his car, and slammed the door behind him. Turning his radio way down, he started driving home, thinking about what just happened.

He'd left in the middle of an interrogation to go to the hospital and speak to a victim. It was important to get there quickly because the nightmare was still fresh in their minds.

He should have called ahead. He shouldn't have left the interrogation. Of course he'd arranged for someone else to make sure Raine and Arie got home all right, but that wasn't the point. Raine Walsh was getting Megan to speak. And that was important in the prison case. Not only that, he should have waited to take Raine with him to the hospital. She could have been helpful. He hadn't been thinking. Details were getting muddled together.

And when things got muddled, he made mistakes.

He was sloppy.

He needed a break.

The smell of apricot and seasoned chicken filled the air as he took the steps up to his apartment. He closed his eyes a moment and inhaled; his stomach grumbled. He was so glad that Ben was the chef in their partnership. He hated cooking. If it were up to him, it'd be tacos from the shack down the road every night. He put his key in the door and twisted it open, pushing into their apartment.

There was a fire in the grate, giving a warm glow to the open floor plan loft. The small butcher block table was set for two. Something that appeared to the remnants of dinner was still on the table.

He quietly set his keys on the counter and walked to the table. Lifting one of the wine glasses to examine it, he saw a smeared lip print, and drop of pink liquid pooled in the bottom.

Benjamin had company.

He heard a faint sound. A murmur coming from the bedroom. Anxiety swelled in his chest. Something wasn't right about this. He turned around and saw a trail of clothing. To his bedroom door. A shirt. A pair of pants. Boxer briefs.

His anxiety burst into a multitude of emotions that overwhelmed him. He could turn around now. He didn't need to see any more.

Or did he? Benjamin wouldn't do something like this. They'd talked about being exclusive. Being loyal. Maybe even starting a family.

He strode to the bedroom door and yanked it open.

The two men leaped apart as though each thought the other was on fire. Benjamin stood at the side of the bed, naked. The brunette with the defined abs reached for a blanket to cover himself.

Jonah spoke before they could start. He pointed at Benjamin. "Don't you dare say 'this isn't what it looks like.'"

"I—I wasn't. Jonah…"

He exited the room that smelled like sweat and sex, and hurried to the kitchen to get his keys.

"Jonah! You weren't supposed to be home tonight!"

"OH, so THAT makes it acceptable? Not getting caught? How are we supposed to start a family if you can't even keep it in your pants? Hm? Am I not good enough for you, Ben?" It was a rhetorical question. He didn't want to know the answer.

"You're always working. I feel like you don't even give me the time of day. I can't marry you, because you're already married to your job! And forget including me—office parties? Ha! How would you like your coworkers actually knowing you prefer men?"

"Nice. That's it right there. That's the justification." He dropped his arms and his hand brushed the badge in his pocket. His eyes began to well up. He stood there, tapping his badge. The badge that gave him superiority, authority, and strength, now made him feel small. "Boundaries, Ben. I hope dinner was good for you and Mr. Eight Abs in there."

"Jonah! Where are you going?"

Jonah yanked the door open and slammed it behind him.

The taco shack down the street was calling his name.

With tacos in his belly, he pulled into a parking lot that overlooked a beach trail. Many years ago, this parking lot hadn't been here. When he was younger, he and his friends would climb down the makeshift staircase cut in the stone. At the bottom were the remains of the old Sutro Baths, a public pool from the early 1900s. The baths were lost to a terrible fire, sometime in the 50s he thought, though there were still people today that remembered going there when they were kids. Nobody knows what started the fire.

When Jonah was a kid, the ruins were a place to drink beer without getting caught, before heading over to Ocean Beach to have a bonfire in the sand. As an adult, it was more than that. It still posed a great mystery to him, and his profession was strictly mysteries. It comforted him to come up here to look out at the ocean and think.

Just in the past few years, commercialism had overtaken the old Sutro Baths. This was no doubt due to the number of tourists that would climb down the dangerous rocks to explore the ruins. Whether there were barricades or not, the tourists would ignore them to see the ocean smashing against the rocks. Cement replaced the original stairs cut into the cliff and led up to a paved parking lot. There was a museum adjacent to the parking lot, selling mugs and reprints of advertisements for special nights at the baths in their heyday. It was cool, but it diminished the authenticity of the place. If it had just been left alone...

Tonight, he'd stay here. He wasn't going back to that tainted apartment. He rested his face in his hands on the steering wheel.

Benjamin... He loved him. But this wasn't the first time he'd walked in on him.

Is it my fault? I'm a workaholic. He could attribute that to his father, who was a cop before him. His job *was* demanding, and the expectations were high.

He knew that when we got together! Benjamin was the kind of man that wasn't ready to settle down, but pretended he was because that's what Jonah wanted. Jonah was a monogamous kind of person. He wasn't sure where they'd go from here. Wherever it was, he didn't feel like dealing with it now.

He jumped when the phone vibrated.

Composing himself, he answered, "Detective Heely."

"Hello sir, this is SF General Hospital, the victim is awake and is in stable condition. He's actually asking to speak to the police. You'd better get down here."

"On my way."

SEVEN

Vinnie

Vinnie's car sat parked on the entrance ramp that led to the interstate. He'd chosen a stretch of highway that was bordered by trees that thickened into a forest.

The sky had already dimmed toward darkness, and he had to strain to see the item he'd planted near the edge of the forest.

He watched as car after car passed by at high speeds, and wondered if the item was visible enough. He took his hands off the steering wheel and looked at them in the blue light. They were clammy and shaking, cold sweat on his palms and at his hairline.

The nerves built up inside him and began to eat away. This was a risk. This time, out of desperation, he'd chosen to find his victim in a less than familiar way. He was breaking his routine. Although he decided that was better because then it made the crimes even more random, and harder to connect.

His eyes pierced the passing cars, and just as he was stifling a yawn, a dark car pulled off to the side of the road. The emergency flashers came on.

Butterflies filled Vinnie's stomach as if he were on his way to meet a woman for a first date. He put his car in drive, checked for oncoming traffic, and eased down the ramp. When he pulled up behind the other car, he flicked on his four-ways as well. The other driver was already at the edge of the woods, examining the item Vinnie planted.

Vinnie pressed the cool metal blade against his hip-bone, sleeked his hair back over his ears with his clammy palms, and pushed open the door. The sound of passing cars was enough to mask the closing of the door, as well as his footsteps as he approached the man.

He was crouched by an infant car seat, covered by a blanket.

"Car troubles?" Vinnie asked, his voice unusually na-sally.

The man jumped and stood up to face Vinnie. "Naw, man. There was this car seat here on the side of the road. I didn't know what to think. I've got two kids at home so I couldn't just drive by."

Vinnie looked down at the car seat, then back at the man.

The man picked up the blanket and dropped it in the grass. "It's empty."

"I know." Vince pursed his lips when his left eyelid twitched.

"Huh?" The man backed up. "You know?"

Vinnie stepped into his personal space and smirked. "Yeah. I put it there." He swiftly pulled the knife and thrust it into the man's abdomen.

He doubled over.

Vinnie twisted it inside him, and he dropped to the ground. It had been easy to catch him off guard. Out of his peripheral vision he saw a car pull in front of the other man's. *Shit*. Vinnie pushed the man's face into his knees so his vision and hearing were impaired.

The window rolled down. "Everything okay?"

"Oh yeah! Thanks! We're all good here; I'm calling for a tow. It's fine."

As the Samaritan rolled their window back up, the man started to thrash in the tall grass.

Vinnie pulled the knife out and the victim struggled to his feet.

"Please," he breathed. "I have a family. Young kids. They need me."

It was as if he was wrapped in a cocoon. Vinnie thought he heard something about kids, but it was distant. He was experiencing a fit of blurry rage and embarrassment, feelings that were resurfacing from a memory he could never escape. A painful memory that made him this way. This man needed to die.

He turned the man around towards the forest. When he tensed like he was going to run, Vinnie stabbed him again. And again. Hidden now by the tree line, nobody would see him stabbing the life out of this innocent guy who stopped to make sure an abandoned baby was safe.

He stabbed him until his rattling breath stopped.

Vinnie moved out of the tree line as if it was the most normal thing, as if he was just taking a piss because he couldn't hold it until the next stop. On his way back to the car, he picked up the car seat. Gwen wouldn't be happy if he lost it. How would he explain that?

He tossed it in the back seat. He closed the door, slipped the knife out, leaned down and thrust the blade into the passenger side tire. It was harder to pull out than it was to pierce. After he yanked it out, the tire began to lose pressure.

Then he went to the victim's car. He jumped into the driver's seat and started it with keys he'd taken from the body. It smelled faintly like Old Spice deodorant.

He tried to remember what the man said before he went down. The words remained muffled, as if his brain had jumbled everything. But he had to follow the routine.

He drove the car all the way home and pulled into the driveway. He hopped out and punched in the code to open the bay of the single car garage. He pulled the car inside, closing the door behind him.

When he went inside the house, the television was blaring, but there was no sign of Gwen or Scarlett. They had to be here, because he had their only car, and she hadn't told him she was going anywhere this evening. She could be putting Scarlett down.

"Gwen!" he yelled.

"Yeah?"

The voice came from their bedroom. She peeked her head out, the baby balanced on one arm, her face pushed against Gwen's bare breast.

"Can you call a tow truck to go pick up our car?"

"Where's our car?" she asked, irritated.

"Flat tire. It's on the side of the interstate. I'm gonna be in the garage for a minute, I'll be in soon. Could you just call for me, please?"

She sighed. "Fine, Vin."

He'd turned back toward the garage when she shouted, "Hey, how'd you get home?"

"Good Samaritan." He slammed the door shut before she could ask any more questions.

He hurried to his workbench and pulled open a drawer. There was a stack of license plates inside. He grabbed one and reached for a screwdriver.

He pried the current plate off of the car, then tilted it back and forth, studying the numbers—the numbers that led him to this situation. Flashes of humiliation, doubt, and utter betrayal filled the void inside his body.

His hands began to tremble, and the license plate clattered to the floor. The sound shattered him. He grabbed at his ears, the ears that were too far from his hairline, more prominent from slicking his black hair behind them.

As fast as the moment came, it was gone again. He scooped up the old license plate, and lifting the false bottom from another drawer, slipped the plate into the space underneath, on top of the others.

Using the same screws, he put the new license plate on the vehicle. He repeated the procedure on the back. Then he opened the garage door, grabbed the keys from the workbench, and hopped in.

He backed it out and parked it few houses up from his and across the street, near a house that always had different cars going in and out of it. After he ditched the keys down the sewer grate, he headed home. He peeled off his sweaty shirt and tossed it into the corner, by some firewood. He'd need to come back later and dispose of it when he had more time. Nobody would be looking into his garage right now, anyway.

Nobody would suspect he left the car there, because nobody noticed suspicious behavior when done with confidence. And though confidence wasn't always Vinnie's strong suit, he was able to pull it off when everything depended on it. He went into the house and headed for the bedroom. Gwen was in Scarlett's room.

"Shower" he shouted and went into the bathroom.

What was done, was done.

EIGHT

Raine

Raine was filling Viona's water bowl when the doorbell rang. She jumped, still not used to the sound of Marcus's doorbell.

She opened the door to the lanky, ashen-haired boy standing there, and motioned him in.

"Hey Vee! Hey girl." He knelt down and greeted her, laughing as she licked his face. He used the back of his sleeve to wipe the slobber from his cheek.

"Where's Marcus?" he asked, as he sat in the navy armchair.

"He went to play racquetball with a friend."

"Ah cool, I've never tried that. Not many racquetball courts in Palo Alto."

"That you know of. You're so busy anyway. How are things going at the shelter?"

"Oh, great. Adopted out nine dogs this past weekend. It was a good turnout."

"That's wonderful! Do you want something to drink?"

"Water's good," he responded.

She went to the kitchen and fixed them each a glass of iced water. She handed one to Arie, and he said, "So lets get down to business."

47

"Aw, you don't want to just hang out?" she asked, half teasing. They were going to have to talk about it sooner or later. "Well what do you want to talk about first? I feel like there's so much to cover."

"Lets talk about your new job first. I didn't even realize you were doing it until we went to talk to... her." He looked down.

She studied his body language.

He was tapping his foot on the floor, his knee bouncing rapidly. He couldn't sit still. "I don't think you owe me a play-by-play, Raine. But this? Man, this is big."

She nodded. "I know. But what else was I going to do, Arie? I haven't even gotten to tell Marcus about this yet. Honestly though, he'd probably be happy I'm working in the field instead of just sitting in my office filing paperwork all day. I want to get back into it. I miss it. I miss talking with clients. I feel like I should be using my—*our* experience to help people."

"Who're you helping, exactly?"

"Well there's another string of murders happening right now. There are some similarities, and they think it might be related to our case."

"How so?"

"Well, they think the underlying psychology might be the same. They're thinking this person, this killer, is us- ing psychological tactics to stay under the radar and not get caught. All of his killings that they know of have been in public. And they found the last victim's car in circumstances very similar to mine."

"Do they think this case has something to do with the Warden?"

"They're not sure, but it's a possibility. We know he's still out there, even though some of the department believes Megan was the mastermind and acted alone."

There was a silence between them as memories flooded back. Anxiety and desperation. There wasn't a day that went by she didn't think about what happened in that prison, or what happened to Troy right in front of her. There wasn't a night that she didn't wake up in a cold sweat with the sound of prison alarms blaring in her mind.

She looked up at Arie, the boy she'd come to admire. But every time she looked at him, the memories resurfaced. It was still strange to see him wearing a t-shirt and hoodie, instead of looking vulnerable in a dirty hospital gown. But every time she thought she couldn't see him again, they shared a moment of mutual understanding. He was the only one who could, and she needed that. "Do you have dreams—nightmares about the alarms?" she asked.

"Oh, yes. Almost every night, Raine. I was in that place for a so long, I'd lost track. Nobody was looking for me because there was no reason to. Nobody was looking for you because they thought you were dead. I was trapped in this prison, not just the psychopath's prison, but also the prison of my social status and the culture I grew up in. I wanted to leave all that and be what I wanted to be, or even just have a chance in life. So when I woke up in that jail, I thought I belonged there. I thought it was destined to happen. And at least my parents didn't have to bail me out. Nobody looked for me because they knew I'd be gone one day. They were hoping I would be."

Raine reached for her water and drank half the glass, wondering what to say. She shook her head, but Arie was rubbing Viona's belly and didn't see. Viona was always a comfort. Her intuition was impeccable, and she always knew who needed her most.

Raine reached out to touch Arie's knee, but thought better of it. Instead, she offered, "Maybe you were meant to be there..."

Arie stiffened.

49

"...because you were meant to meet me. If we hadn't been taken, we never would have met each other, and we wouldn't be sitting here now."

"You're great at talking, you know that?" His voice was gruff, but he smiled slightly.

She shrugged.

"That's why you need to help Heely with this case. You belong in the 'helping people' department."

She stifled a laugh. "How did it—never mind..." She cut herself off and scanned the apartment to find a distraction.

"What?"

"Never mind."

"Naw, you can't do that, you started to say something. Just spit it out, it's okay."

She sighed. "How did it feel to see Meg?" she asked.

There was a moment of tense silence, and Raine, appalled by what she'd said, wanted to turn on the TV for some white noise, something distracting.

"It felt like lots of things. I play it over and over in my head. I think about how she deceived us. But then, I think about her own ordeal."

All Raine could think about was that the girl tried to kill her. She'd given Megan the benefit of the doubt. Stockholm syndrome. Trapped. Megan had even made it appear that she wanted to help rescue them. But she'd helped the Warden escape, then she went to the hospital to kill Raine. Raine didn't feel the same things for Megan that Arie did.

"I know what you're thinking."

She cocked an eyebrow at him.

He continued, "But I don't believe her lies anymore. Yes, of course I had a different relationship with her than you did. She was my only friend in there, my only hope for a long time. But when I heard her from behind the mirror, I saw who she really is. It gave me the motivation to get out there and track down the Warden. He's out there. We know it. I don't think the cops are looking hard enough. I think they think that Megan is it. That she was behind it and there's nobody else to catch. They have evidence she'd been stealing drugs from the hospital she worked at. I think they think she drugged us into thinking there was someone else. But you and I both know Megan wasn't capable of pulling off that entire operation."

"Right. We were both there. We know what happened. But I saw something else in Megan. Yes, she was meek and sensitive, but I could see the deception in her eyes. It was terrifying."

Arie nodded. "My point is, do you want to help me find the Warden?"

Her eyes widened. "Of course. Do you have a place to start?"

"You have direct access to our case. The police officer-now-detective, Detective Jonah Heely, is at your beck and call."

She thought about that. "What do you suggest I do? Don't you think he'll realize what I'm doing?"

"I'm sure you can think of something."

Raine nodded. She started to get excited about the possibility of learning more, then she laughed and shook her head.

"What?"

"You and your plans."

"But they always work out."

"I wouldn't necessarily say *that*."

"Would you say it's worth a try?"

Raine nodded. "Of course."

Raine rolled over under the navy duvet and opened her eyes. Marcus was sleeping soundly. She watched his bare chest rise and fall in the sunlight from the crack in the curtains.

He was her constant in times of change, ever since she moved to San Francisco. They'd been friends for a long time before she realized he was the right person for her, even though he'd been entranced from the moment they met. She fought it for a long time, until she realized that a relationship with him was right.

As she worked through the memories, they had their own issues to work through. She'd told him all about Arie.

She couldn't blame herself for the feelings she had for Arie when they were imprisoned, and because of the circumstances. Marcus didn't blame her either. He was too skilled a psychologist to not understand.

She watched him sleep, grateful to him. Because he was so mentally strong, a natural caregiver. She wanted to lean over and kiss him, but it was time for her to get up, and she didn't want to wake him.

Her thoughts shifted to the day ahead. She had an appointment with Detective Heely.

She was able to get ready without waking Marcus. She showered, dressed quietly, and left the bedroom, closing the door behind her.

As she made a pot of coffee, Viona was bouncing around her feet in excitement.

"Quiet Vee," she whispered and reached for her keys. She opened the door and let Viona out. The pit mix was so well behaved that she didn't need a leash to go out and do her business, though Raine carried one anyway for appearances.

After Viona finished, Raine led her back and locked her inside, then she flipped her sunglasses down over her eyes and headed for her car.

NINE

Detective Heely

Jonah gulped his water as if he couldn't get enough of it. His gaze was fixed on the corkboard in the conference room. Each conference room in the building had a huge corkboard for mapping out cases. He was currently using one for the stabbing serial case he was working on. He had pictures of each victim on a detailed map of the city: the construction site, an apartment lobby, the side of the highway.

That last one was puzzling. The killer no doubt thought the man was dead. Jonah mulled it over for the hundredth time.

This one was different from the other two killings. The other two were done openly, disregarding potential witnesses. Witnesses? They were just bystanders.

Jonah even began to call him the Bystander Killer, though only to himself. He didn't want the media picking up on it, because they sensationalized everything. He wanted to keep this as quiet as possible, because publicity could be what this particular killer thrived on. Was the killer in some sort of public occupation? A news anchor? A grocery clerk?

He grabbed a pen and started scrawling occupations that fit his theory.

Back to the case, Jonah. He circled back to the three victims. This third case, though it was done with the same weapon, didn't make sense. It was off. It didn't follow this guy's pattern. Doubt tugged at him. He needed to consider all the possibilities.

He rubbed his temples as a minor headache emerged. This was familiar, his thinking headache. Puzzles were his whole job. He enjoyed it, but it was frustrating when he couldn't catch a break.

Voices in the hall caught his attention and he leaned out of the conference room. His office door was open. Wondering what was up, he went to his office and found Raine waiting for him.

"Raine?" he asked.

She turned in her chair and smiled at him.

"I'm so glad you're here." He'd almost forgotten he asked her to come in for another briefing.

He sat down at his desk, and shuffled some papers. He made a mental note to organize paperwork later. Again. Something he probably wasn't going to do anyway.

"What I mean is, I'm happy you've decided to take this on, after everything you went through."

She crossed her legs. "You know, I haven't seen clients since my accident. I still go to work, of course, for normalcy, but I was about ready to get back into it. Then you approached me to help with this."

He interjected, "I told you that you could back out at any time."

"I know. But I'm fine. I'm trying to tell you that this case is helping me get back into my profession."

"I also told you that if you help with this case, I'd give you access to the prisoner. And that could help close your case too, and I know you want that."

She nodded. "There's something in it for both of us."

He nodded, unsure where to take this next. He looked at her thoughtfully, then retrieved a binder from a desk drawer. "I was hoping you'd be able to talk to the man we think is a survivor of the Bystander Killer. He could have the answers we need to find this guy. You're the right person for this."

"Yes, we all know how your bedside manner is." She laughed softly.

"We do? No we don't. What's my bedside manner like?"

She laughed again. "Don't you recall our first meeting, Detective Heely? In the hospital..."

He nodded. *Oh, yeah. That.* "I did forget about that. That was back in my uniform days. I was the one there after you woke up. I was only there to take notes. I'm sure this victim has already given a statement. I'm on this case to work the details. It's a little bit different. But anyway, listen. The part that I really can't understand is that this killer is taking victims at random, or it at least appears that way."

"He wasn't in my case."

"You know why Warden took you?"

"I believe he took people that he felt were indirectly related to murders. I never murdered anyone. But I blamed myself for a client's suicide a few years ago."

"I see. Well the first step is to have you meet the victim, and we can go from there."

"That sounds good—" A loud bang from the lobby cut her off.

"What the hell!" Jonah leapt up from his desk and threw open the door. There was a man leaning over the reception the counter with his fists clenched. He turned and looked at Jonah.

The man's face was familiar, but he couldn't place it.

He didn't need to.

Raine pushed past him and said, "Marcus? What in the world?"

"I've been calling you!" he shouted, his face going from anger to relief and back.

She pulled her phone out of her bag. "I—I'm sorry, I must have had my phone on silent. Is every—are you okay?"

"I was so goddamn worried about you! You can't do that to me. I woke up and you were gone. I thought you'd already gone to the office. I get to the office and you're not there! After everything you and I just went through..."

Raine raised her hand to quiet him, her face blank.

"Whoa! Do you two need a moment alone? You can't just come in here slamming doors and shouting!" Jonah said.

"It's okay. I'll—Marcus let's go out to the car. Jonah, I'll be right back, okay?"

He nodded. Raine hooked her arm in Marcus's and dragged him towards the exit.

Was he a controlling boyfriend? Raine seemed to manage him, seemed confident. But he could definitely see Marcus being the controlling type, despite his profession. Raine had been with him so long that maybe she didn't recognize his manipulation?

Who the hell am I judging? he thought to himself. *Manipulation?* If anyone had experience in relationship manipulation, it was him. He had Benny. He'd just caught Benjamin in his bed with another man. And it wasn't the first time. And he kept going back. Why? *Because I always blame myself?*

He was too dedicated to his work. He was always missing plans. *Did I drive him to cheat?*

Yeah, Raine would have to work this one out on her own. He went back into his office and sat down at his desk.

And hopefully she worked it out soon. He didn't have all day.

TEN

Vinnie

Saturday. It was the best day of the week because he didn't have to go to work. He didn't have to go in on Sunday either, but Sunday reminded him of the impending doom that waited for him on Monday. He enjoyed the few minutes of peace before a piercing scream erupted from the family room. Vinnie didn't even so much as flinch at the sound, though his eye twitched. He could usually tune out the twitch, but this time he reached up to the side of his eye and held it. Another piercing scream.

He sighed and maneuvered off the mattress. Wearing only his boxers, he walked over to his dresser and yanked out a black v-neck shirt to put on. He walked down the hallway and into the kitchen.

"Vinnie, I think she has an ear infection again. She's just so fussy." His wife had the baby on her hip, bouncing her up and down. The family room was trashed with toys.

He turned away from them and stared at the mountainous pile of dishes in the sink. He thought about bitching about Gwen not doing housework—heaven forbid she take two seconds to wash a plate or a dish.

Gwen spent all her time at home with Scarlett, and she still couldn't get the housework done so that he could relax at home. He looked back at her, her hair stringy and dark bags under her eyes. She bounced the blubbering, snot-nosed, red-faced baby with her eyes glued to the TV. She glanced at him and back to the television again. "You see this, Vin?"

He looked at the TV, the volume low with the subtitles on. It was the morning news, though it must have been a recording because they didn't air the morning news on weekends. Gwen had a tendency to record things because she wasn't able to watch when tending to the baby.

His heart skipped a beat when he saw the news anchor standing in front of a line of trees. His body tensed. "You don't need to be watching this garbage." He held out his arms to take the baby from his wife.

She handed her off.

He moved the baby to his shoulder and put a burp towel under Scarlett's wet chin.

Gwen slumped, her eyes exhausted.

"Has she been awake all night?" he asked, watching the news out of the corner of his eye.

She nodded.

"Why don't you go take a shower? Take your time, enjoy it."

"Seriously?" She sounded surprised.

"Yes, seriously! You deserve it!"

She laughed, clearly charmed by his words. "Okay. But if she starts fussin' I've got extra bottles of breast milk in the fridge and you'll want to warm—"

"I got it." His voice came out sterner than he meant it to, though she laughed like he'd made a joke. He didn't. He needed her to get the hell out of the room right now. Anything could come up on that TV.

She didn't even get halfway down the hall before he shouted, "Shit!"

"What's wrong?"

The headline on the news said that a killer was at large but they didn't have much information. I mean, it could have been any killer, right? What were the odds? Of course the odds had never been on his side. "Oh nothing. Scarlett threw up on me," he replied.

She laughed. "Try staying at home one of these days and see how often you're thrown up on." She slammed the bedroom door.

"Well, somebody needs to provide for this family. It's not like we'll ever win the lottery," he muttered. He picked up Gwen's coffee, and took a sip. "Uck!" He put the cold coffee down and sat on the sofa with Scarlett on his knee.

She seemed content for the moment, and he used the towel on his shoulder to wipe her mouth and nose, even though it was a lost cause. His eyes were glued to the news.

They were reporting on a case where a man was *nearly* stabbed to death.

Vinnie did a double take. Nearly. Nearly stabbed to death. Not actually stabbed to death. The man lived.

It couldn't be his man. His victims never lived. He couldn't even be sure this case had anything to do with him. Generally he was very disoriented from the adrenaline of satisfying the urge. But he didn't make mistakes. He didn't leave tracks.

But this last urge was different from the rest.

This one didn't follow his pattern. And this one was messy.

He figured it'd be good to throw off any authorities that might be connecting things, but he really didn't do much thinking about it at all. He needed to stop the urges that overcame him. He had no choice. After the kill, or what he thought was a kill, he did his ritual cover up with the plates on the car.

The car.

He slipped the cooing baby onto the couch and leaped to the window. He pulled back the powder blue curtains and saw the car still sitting there, sporting shiny new plates.

He looked back over in time to see Scarlett rolling to the edge of the couch. He scooped her back up, then slumped on the couch with her on his lap. He looked at the TV again. Commercials. When the news came back, they were showing the Powerball drawing.

The searing white balls with bold black numbers filled the screen. A fire rose up inside him.

This was it. The lottery numbers. It wasn't even in real time. These were last night's numbers, but this segment of the news set him off every time, surfacing feelings imploding only to surface again. He couldn't take it. He couldn't handle it.

He heard the screech of pipes and water rushing to the shower.

He started to feel woozy, and leaned back on the couch.

Shit. Shit. It's happening. It's not even the real broadcast, he thought to himself. The lottery numbers hammered his brain. He could turn it off. Right? Yeah, he could turn it off.

Only it was too late. Holding Scarlett was almost too much. He put her in her swing, then started the thing without the lullaby music. The music killed him. It was repetitive and skipped in and out. It was a bargain they found at a thrift store.

Now that the baby was out of his arms, he fumbled for the remote and shut off the TV. Then he plopped back on the couch and reached up to his face, clawing at his eyes.

The episode was already upon him. He had to take it as it sunk its teeth down on his mind, disabling him entirely. He relived the moment again. The moment of humiliation. The moment of sheer horror. The worst feeling he'd experienced in his life.

His mind drifted back to a time marked by his buzzed head and the fact that his recently knocked up wife held onto his arm. Her off the shoulder red velvet dress was as riveting as her matching red lipstick. He wore a shitty blazer his Mom gave him that used to be his father's—one of those tweed ones with the elbow patches that didn't match. One you'd find with moth holes in the sleeves. There probably were.

Gwen looked nice. Gwen fit in. She was social and sweet, and he had no idea how he landed her back in college. He must have been easy. Well, he *was* easy. He wouldn't leave her, and she knew it, and used it to her advantage. But she was always faithful. She was from a small town, one of those places you only married once and you had children right away and the woman is the homemaker.

He pulled the ribbon off the package in front of him, and opened the box to find two scratch-off tickets inside.

"Come on, Vinnie, see if you're a winner!" One of his coworkers shouted from the back.

"Naw, guys. I'll just scratch um when I get home, it's okay. Thanks, really thoughtful." He pasted a smile on his face.

"Scratch them now, everyone's watching." Gwen nudged his arm.

His face and neck grew hot, and he didn't dare look up at everyone staring at him, excited about the gift. Christmas parties were always like this. So awkward. Everyone watches as you open your present and judges you based on your reaction. The entire thought of gift giving was awkward and filled him with anxiety.

But fine, he'd scratch the ticket for their entertainment.

He reached into his pocket and pulled out his keys. He put the tickets down on the table.

There were a lot of people at the DMV party. The annual holiday party included every branch in the city. It was always the same thing: some shitty rented out gym or cafeteria, with plastic tablecloths taped to the tables. They'd cater in a dinner of some sort and do a secret Santa gift exchange.

Gwen got a candle and a bottle of wine that she wouldn't be able to drink anyway due to the pregnancy.

He pressed the key on the card and scratched, following the directions. "I won two bucks!" He stood up and showed the card. That was enough of a win to break even, pay back the money it cost for the card itself. He set down the winner and looked at the other card. At this point, people were starting to move on with their conversations. Light jazz holiday music was playing over the loudspeaker. There were far more interesting things to engage in than watching a desk agent scratch off a lottery ticket.

He pressed the key into the foil and scratched each box, each revealing a number he needed.

That's how those things always work. You get down to the very last number, getting your hopes and adrenaline up, and then the last number is wrong. It's all part of the game. He scratched and scratched, dragging his wrist against the table. Sure enough, the numbers were matching up.

He got down to the last one, and scratched.

Holy shit. "Gwen, are you seeing what I'm seeing?" he asked, not taking his eyes off the winning numbers. He shoved it over at her. She scanned the card, her eyes widening. She looked up at him. "It's a joke, right?"

He looked around the room and back down at the card. "We won? It's a joke, it has to be a joke. Tell me!" he shouted and jumped up. The plastic folding chair crashed to the ground and people turned to watch.

"I won! Five hundred grand! Are you serious?" His whole body tensed from his toes to his head. His hands began to shake as he grabbed the card and waved it in the air. He put it down on the table. People gasped and applauded, someone clapping him on the back.

He turned to look at his newly pregnant wife, tears in his eyes. "We just won half a million dollars!" His voice squeaked and he reached up and swiped the back of his hands at both eyes, overwhelmed and overcome with emotion.

Thoughts shot through his head faster than a bullet.

I could quit my deadbeat job.

I could pay all our overdue bills.

I could free myself of our debt.

I could pay for a nursery.

I could take her out to dinner! A lot of dinners!

His life would change from this point forward.

"Did you read the instructions on the back, Vinnie? Read the directions!" someone shouted.

Laughter rippled around the room.

"I won!" he squeaked again. He turned the card over "Read the rules!"

He could hardly see the words. His hands were shaking, his mind racing. He needed to calm down so he could concentrate and see what he needed to do next to claim the prize.

The words didn't make sense. There were no directions to claim the prize. There were a few insulting sentences—a prank.

"It's a joke?" he asked, his face red and blotchy.

"Yeah, man! We got you!" Heckling laughter erupted, sounding like hyenas.

He looked over at Gwen, who seemed to just be grasping the situation, and she patted the back of Vinnie's jacket.

"Nice prank, guys. Very funny," she said in her matter-of-fact tone, her hand on her hip, and a smirk on her lips.

She didn't know about it.

"Ah shit. You're all in on this?" he asked.

His heart thrummed against the inside of his chest, humiliation rising up inside him. His throat tightened, and his mind began to cave in on itself.

He felt a tap on his arm as his wife got swept up in a crowd of women. A crowd formed around him as well, and coworkers laughed in slow motion, asking him if he thought it was real, and asking him what he'd do with the money. They laughed in his face and laughed at his expense. *They knew. They all knew.*

He couldn't leave, because everyone's eyes continued to bore into him. Taunting him. He wanted to disappear. How could he face these people again after tonight? But he had no choice. He was the only one that could provide for his family, for his wife and unborn child.

So he put on a face. A facade. It was all he could do. He chuckled when somebody yelled, "You take things so seriously!"

He let out a laugh, grabbed the wine glass off the table and took a swig. That's what people did at these functions, right? They drank until their heads spun. They screwed their hot, tipsy, coworker against the bathroom sink. And they played god-awful mean pranks on the people they didn't like. He could play that game.

He'd played it his whole life. He played that game since fourth grade when he'd come home from school to an empty house with an empty fridge. He knew that game all too well. Act like them. Function like them. Survive like them.

"Gwen!" he shouted, putting up his hand to motion for his wife. "Excuse me," he said to Stan after reading the "Hello my name is" sticker on his chest. Stan must have been an agent from another branch.

He walked toward his wife and put his hand on the small of her back, leaning in and saying, "I need to use the restroom. I'll be right back."

She nodded, her red lips parting into a smile, one front tooth snagged in such a cute, homely way.

Then he turned towards the glaring exit sign over the door, and narrowed his vision.

When he reached the bathroom and realized nobody was there, he closed the door and locked it. There were three stalls and three adjacent urinals, but he wanted the whole place to himself. When the lock clicked he went to the sink and peered at himself in the mirror.

He looked for two seconds before he lost it.

Pressure built up behind his eyes, and streams of tears slipped down his jawline. His breath was heaving, all while he kept it as quiet as he could. He cupped his hands over his eyes and pressed. He wanted to rip his skin off.

Then something inside him told him to let it go. It wasn't his fault. It was theirs. It was the fault of those that laughed at his expense. They'd tricked him. It was as though everyone was out to get him. To make him feel, for one split second in time, that maybe his life could be an ounce less shitty. Yes, he was stupid for believing that something that good could or would happen to him by luck or chance. But it was their fault for making him feel the way he felt now.

And somebody would have to pay for that.

He recalled the feeling of holding the ticket in his hand and thinking that in that moment, his whole life had changed.

That feeling wasn't wrong. His whole life HAD changed from that moment forward. The lottery was the trigger.

ELEVEN

Raine

Raine leaned against Marcus's tiny, beat up car and crossed her arms over her chest. "I should have told you I was working with this detective. I only just decided it was something I could help with, and we haven't had a chance to sit down and talk about it."

Marcus reached up and scratched his head, hair buzzed into a thin layer of black fuzz. "I'm not mad at you for taking this job, Raine."

She looked up at him. "You are mad, though."

"I'm upset because I didn't know where you were. I want you to live your life. But we've been through this before. Where I go to work and you don't show up. And then I'm told you're dead. I didn't know where you were this morning and you weren't answering your phone. For all I knew, you could have been gone again or in danger. They never caught the person that took you."

"I know. I'm sorry. I should keep my phone on. And what you just said there, that they haven't actually caught the Warden, well that's one of the reasons I chose to help this detective. He thinks our cases are connected in some way. Or have some sort of parallel. We don't—" She looked around the parking lot. "We don't have to discuss it here." Marcus put his hand on her arm.

"I'm happy you want to use your talent to help others. I'm proud of you."

Even after she was the jerk and didn't answer his calls when he worried about her, he still showed compassion. "Well I appreciate you. You've stepped up and taken on the majority of my clients."

"You know I don't mind. We should really consider starting to take some interviews to fill the third spot in our office. Maybe you could go back to Stanford and put up signs. Talk to our old professors about whether they know anybody good that would be interested. We can talk about this later, too."

She nodded. It was bittersweet. She loved the idea of a new beginning. It would be kind of nice to go back to the university she graduated from to see if they could give her any referrals.

But then on the other side of the new beginning was the end they were leaving behind. She'd never forget what happened to Troy. Never. And his death was the reason they needed to hire another counselor for the practice.

"Anyway, I don't want to keep you. Just, communicate, okay? I love you."

She nodded and smiled, and pecked his lips with her own. "I will. Again, I'm sorry." She turned to go.

"One more thing."

She looked back at him.

"Did you have a guy over last night?" he asked.

"Arie." She tipped her head to inquire. "How'd you—"

"The toilet seat was up when I got home. It's okay, I was just curious."

"Mm.... See you later, Marcus." She smiled and went back inside.

She respected that he loved and cared for her, and that it had been hell when he thought she died, but it was hard for her to have to answer to someone. When she moved into his apartment, she gave up a huge part of her independence. She missed that. Not that she didn't enjoy being with Marcus, nor did she mind that he wanted to take care of her, but hadn't she proven to herself that it was up to her to take care and survive?

Raine pushed through the door of Detective Heely's office and shut it behind her. She put her purse on the ground and plopped in the seat across from his desk.

"Everything okay?" he asked her.

"Yeah, of course. He's just worried about me. I didn't get a chance to tell him I'd decided to work with you guys yet. He was expecting me at the office so when I wasn't there, he had flashbacks from the last time I didn't show up at the office."

He nodded. "Right. So lets' get down to business."

She watched him pull a folder from a pile of paperwork. She thought about saying something about his messy office, but from years of studying psychology and working with patients in a clinical setting, she knew better than to judge. In his mind it could seem organized. Just because it wasn't up to her standards of organization didn't mean it was wrong. And he clearly knew where the folder that he needed was.

"How do you feel your meeting with the perp went?"

"Well, terrible." She laughed, though it wasn't at all funny. "But to be expected. Arie and I believe that she definitely knows where the others are, or where they were taken, but we also got the sense that something terrible has happened to them."

Jonah scribbled something on a legal pad inside the folder.

She wanted to look at the notes he was writing, but once again, she understood. When she was in a counseling session, she tried to keep her note taking to a minimum, or at least as unobtrusive as possible, for reasons exactly like this. The client would think she was judging them, and the whole point was to gain trust.

He looked up at her again. "Right. When we watched later, I got that sense as well. And she hasn't spoken since. But that was a big lead for us, so thank you for going in there. I know it wasn't easy."

She nodded.

"Now, I'd like to talk to you about the next person we need you to speak with."

"Wait, that's it? You aren't going to tell me any details about my case?"

Jonah leaned back in his chair. "Look, Raine. Your case is active, but I do need to focus on this bystander killer case. I have to follow up with that one while it's still fresh."

"The deal was, I help you and you help me."

"Right, but you haven't helped much, now have you?"

She sighed and bit her tongue.

"There's a killer out there right now, as we speak."

"There's more than one." She glared at him.

"Raine. We have Megan. You're safe."

"Megan is not Allen. Allen is the one who kidnapped me, and who knows how many others. Allen was my abuser. He deserves to be locked up, not out there doing whatever he wants. Megan was a conspirator, but I still believe she was manipulated. There are other people out there that still need rescued."

"I understand that. And I vow to you that I will not let your case go cold. But I have to focus on catching this serial stabber out there. And I need your help."

She *did* agree to help. "Who's the next person you want me to speak with?"

"The man that was nearly stabbed to death. He's having trouble talking, but you may be able to get some details."

"Well if you took the same approach with him as you did me, then I don't blame him." She thought she heard him chuckle at that.

"That's why we need your help. Your experience."

"I can talk with him. What exactly are you trying to learn?" she asked.

"We really just need to see how much of the attack he remembers. It's been a few days, and the longer we wait, the longer he has to imagine things and gets less accurate."

Raine nodded. She understood that completely. She recalled a conversation she'd had with Arie, when she shared the experience she had her freshman year of college. She remembered details now that weren't even true. The more time that passed, the more her mind filled in what she thought she experienced. It was a human flaw.

"Detective—"

Raine and Jonah looked toward the door.

"Maxine, I'm in the middle of a meeting here."

"It's okay." Raine said. She saw Maxine and Jonah exchange glances.

The secretary motioned to the phone. "The phone. It's urgent. Want me to put it through?"

Jonah looked down at the phone on his desk, then back up at Raine.

"I can go if you need me to," she said.

He shook his head. "Naw, it's okay, I'll take it in the other room. You stay here and then we can go to the hospital together."

She nodded.

Jonah pushed his chair back.

Her heart began to speed up as she watched him cross the main office and pick up a phone, facing away from her.

She reached forward and slid the folder toward her. She flipped it open. A page of notes. She shuffled through the police and hospital reports.

Come ON! she urged as she leafed through the papers, not finding anything. Was there any sign that they had a lead on the Warden? Were they even looking for him? But as she halfway suspected, she wasn't finding any trace of his existence in the file to begin with. This confirmed her belief that they still thought Megan was the whole operation, and that the rest was something she and Arie had imagined.

She glanced back over her shoulder and froze, Jonah looked he was about to turn around, but then he leaned back down on the desk.

She had no time to think about the close call. She turned the page, and what she saw stunned her.

It was an autopsy report.

And the name on the top of the page sent goose bumps down her arms, and a spear right through her heart.

Shaking, she fumbled in her purse for her phone. She pulled up the camera. She needed to get a photo of this information. Her hands shook and she dropped the phone on the desk with a loud clunk, then looked back at reception.

Jonah was looking straight at her.

Her heart skipped a beat.

He pointed to the phone at his ear and rolled his eyes, unaware of what she was up to. She smiled and he turned away again.

She shook her head and grabbed her phone. She turned it and held it up parallel, snapping a photo of the paperwork.

She was furious at what she saw, but because she couldn't let the detective know she'd been snooping, she needed to keep a wall around her feelings.

If the police weren't going to help her, she'd have to help herself. She'd have to do what she could to help the others. It seemed as though the police were ignoring their existence entirely.

After she got the photo she needed and slammed the folder shut—

"Sorry about that. We're trying to coordinate between two offices and it can get pretty irritating. You ready?" he asked.

She turned to him and nodded, reaching for her purse.

"What's wrong?" he asked.

Her heart skipped a beat. "Huh?"

"You're as white as a ghost."

He surveyed the room. She reached up and brushed her bangs out of her eyes. "Oh, sorry. I haven't eaten all day. I'm just starting to feel it."

"We can grab something on the way to the hospital if you'd like." he said. He started to gather up folders and put them in the drawer to lock up. He stopped when he got to hers.

Her stomach lurched up to her throat.

But then he scooped it up and added it to the others; locking the drawer with a set of keys he kept on his belt loop.

It wasn't until after she was sure he didn't know that she began to wonder. *Why wouldn't he tell her about this?*

She slipped her phone into her purse, the phone that held the revelation securely inside.

The ride from Detective Heely's office to the hospital was an awkward one. She didn't want to talk to him. He was hiding things from her. She couldn't un-see the autopsy report.

They stopped and picked up sandwiches on the way. The cucumber hummus flatbread felt like a lump in her throat. She wasn't hungry at all, but she'd used that excuse so she ate as much as she could before she wrapped it up and stuffed the rest in her purse.

"It's kind of nice having a partner sitting next to me, ya know?" Jonah said.

She winced as his voice cut the silence, and let out a small, airy laugh.

"We *are* allowed to talk to each other," he joked. "I used to have a partner when I was on the street enforcement side. Don't get me wrong; I absolutely love being a detective. Every street cop, well most, hope to become a detective one day. Less grunt work. More in depth cases instead of off the cuff, damage control."

"Don't take offense to my silence, Jonah. My profession is almost entirely talking. So in my downtime, I'm quieter." She tried to hold her voice steady. *Partners, my ass. He's hiding things from me.* At that thought, she felt bad. Guilty. She was wrong to go through his things. *Maybe he was waiting for the right time to tell me?*

"I get that," he answered. "So we don't have to talk about work. How's living with Marcus?" he asked.

"It's okay. I miss my independence sometimes. But it's nice to have somebody worried about you and checking in with you." She was conscious of the fact that Jonah saw the interaction between her and Marcus an hour or so ago. "Earlier, he was just reminding me to keep our communication open. I was wrong not showing up to where he expected me to be and not communicating my change of plans."

"Is he controlling?" Jonah asked.

Raine laughed, cocking an eyebrow. "No. He's a good guy. He was making sure I was safe. When I was taken, he felt a complete loss of control, and that's hard when you love someone. We're not... We're together, yes. But I'm not in any kind of mental state to be in a relationship with someone right now. I'm working out my demons. But enough about me." She was surprised she carried the conversation as far as she did. "Are you seeing someone?" she deflected.

He hesitated. "Kind of?"

"I get that." She laughed. "What's her name?"

"His. The guy I'm seeing's name is Ben."

"I'm sorry. I shouldn't have assumed." She looked into her lap and cursed the gender and sexuality biases she grew up with in Ohio.

"No worries, why would I expect you to just know that?"

"So, Ben. You're *kind of* seeing each other?" she asked.

He hesitated again.

"I'm sorry. You don't have to tell me. It's your personal business."

"I opened this can of worms." He laughed. "Ben has been staying with me, and I do like him. But he's been unfaithful. And more than once. I walked in on him the other day with another guy in my bed, and haven't gone back to the apartment since."

"Where are you staying?" she asked.

"In my car... in my office...."

"Shit, Jonah! It's your place, why don't you kick him out?" She moved forward with emotion, completely blocking out her therapist mindset. She'd almost forgotten the reason they were driving together.

"I don't kick him out because I think I love him. And I think it's my fault. I cancel plans all the time. He's lonely. I'm a workaholic."

"Jonah."

He pulled into a parking spot.

She touched his arm as he looked down at the steering wheel. "It's not your fault. Listen to me."

He looked up at her.

"Ben cheating on you is not your fault. You do not deserve that. You deserve someone who supports you and your work. You deserve someone that won't make you feel guilty for doing what gives you fulfillment in life."

"I know."

"I'm not saying that Ben can't be that person for you, but you guys have some boundaries and things you need to work out. I'm sorry to get so intense but that just floored me." She reached up and smoothed her hair.

"Thanks, Raine."

She nodded. "I'm sorry to get so deep, but that's what happens when I talk with people."

He laughed. "Well let's get back to work."

She got out and slammed the door, while he rounded the vehicle and headed for the hospital building.

"You coming?"

She leaned on the car. "Hey, you go ahead and I'll catch up. I need to make a quick phone call. I'll be right in!"

Jonah nodded and continued towards the building.

Raine watched him for a moment before she reached into her purse and pulled out her phone. She immediately sent the photo she took to Arie, and then clicked on his name to call.

It took a few rings before he picked up. Dogs barked in the background. "What's up? I'm at work."

"This'll be quick." She spoke low and fast.

"Everything okay?" His voice tensed.

"Yes, I think. I'm okay. Uhm, so I just sent you a photo text that you should look at when we get off the phone. I was in Heely's office. He left for a minute and I snooped, like we planned. It's worse than I thought. I can't even say the words aloud. But look at the autopsy report I sent you."

"Autopsy?"

"Just look at it. This is proof that nobody is going to help us. Not law enforcement, not anyone."

"I've been telling you that all along."

"I'm going into a hospital to talk to a victim now, so I can't talk but we can talk about it later. There's an address on there that I'm pretty sure is his family. I'd like to go there. I gotta go, Arie. Talk soon!" She hung up before he could respond. She realized her hands were shaking, and she slipped the phone back in her purse. She needed to get her bearings before she went into the hospital and began working. Working as if nothing had happened or changed since she saw that they had found the body of Brandon Perez.

Raine moved around the different officials and approached the room.

A nurse practitioner stopped her to say, "He's having a good day today, so it's perfect timing to try and ask him about what he remembers. He was in and out of coherency for a while, but we have him on some pain medication that should keep him comfortable."

Raine nodded along, as she listened to what the nurse said.

"If at any time he becomes agitated, I will not hesitate to pull you out."

"I've got this. You don't have to worry." Raine smiled at her. "I'm a professional, and I will not push him. I will see when he's had enough, and he will, because these kinds of conversations are exhausting. I've been there. I know." She thought she saw a hint of a smile on Jonah's lips.

He'd been there too, but in her current role. His face told her he'd been in this position many times.

That thought made her nervous. This was her first encounter with a client that didn't consent to see her first. Not only that, but this visit could also prove her worth to the case. And she wanted to help as much as she could. She thought it was a great idea to bring a therapist on board, instead of trying to hurry the people and victims that could actually help them solve crimes.

The nurse nodded and turned to open the door for Raine.

When she entered the room she peeled off her badge and stuck it in her pocket. It was intimidating to see titles.

She just wanted to have a conversation with him. She crept into the dimly lit room.

The man was sitting in the recliner chair next to the bed, his feet elevated. His auburn hair was bushy on top, and his facial hair had begun to grow in. He was shirtless, with a large white bandage wrapped around his midsection. His hand rested on top of it. A blanket covered his legs.

"Hi there."

His bleary eyes looked away from the television at her, as if he didn't hear her come in. "I thought you were a nurse," he croaked.

"Do you need one?" She motioned to the door.

He shook his head. "Please, no. That means they're either here to poke me, or bring me more nasty food."

Raine stifled a laugh. "Tell me about it. The potatoes are the worst. And don't get me started on whatever it is they're trying to pass for meat." She saw the corner of his lips turn up. "My name is Raine. I'm here to chat with you about what happened, whenever you're ready. But we can just talk about whatever, if you'd like."

"You're a shrink?"

She didn't try to stifle it this time. "You could say that. But not really, I'm a licensed psychologist. But I'm not here to pick your brain. I'm here to try and get some clues about who hurt you. I was in your position not too long ago."

He raised his eyebrow. "You were stabbed?" he asked.

"Not quite. But I was kidnapped, drugged, bound, and caged."

"Damn."

"What's your name?" she asked.

"I'm Kevin."

"Mind if I take a seat, Kevin?" she asked, pointing to the bed.

He nodded his head.

She sat on the edge of his bed facing him. "My abductor was never caught. He's still out there. Like yours. But you're an important part of this. You could help us find your attacker before he hurts anyone else."

"I mean, I'd like to but everything happened so fast. My head is so foggy."

"And the meds probably don't help either. Trust me, I remember."

He smirked. "That's right. I asked them to cut back a bit so I don't become dependent. But my gut is just... ugh."

"I'm sorry." She eyed his bandage. She could almost feel the pain herself.

"Do you want to just go over why you stopped on the side of the highway that night?"

"You're asking me to go back to that night."

Raine looked down. "I understand it's painful to do that. But that man, he has no idea that you're alive. He wanted you dead. He left you for dead. We have to stop him. Let's just try to go back to that night, and if it gets too hard, we can stop at any time, okay?"

He nodded. "I stopped on the side of the highway that night for a baby seat. There's some woods there before the exit, not too far from the side of the highway, and I saw the car seat sitting by the trees. I have two small kids—"

"How old are they?"

He stopped as though it caught him off guard, as though it wasn't relevant, but his face lit up.

Her goal was to get the information she needed without exhausting him. To show him that she cared that he was a human being and not just a victim, the way she felt when she was questioned so many times after her accident. And she genuinely cared about this man and his life. That was the difference between her talking to him, versus law enforcement questioning. They wanted to get straight to the point. Get in, get the answers to the questions, and get out. But that's not how she operated, and if they wanted her involved, and they wanted information on the case, they'd have to be patient.

Time *was* of the essence, but she felt like this was the most efficient way to get what they needed.

"Marley is five, and Jakob is three." He began to get teary-eyed.

"I can tell you love them very much." She smiled at him. "I'm so happy that you're here, Kevin. You beat the odds."

He nodded.

"So you're a caring father, and when you saw that car seat you had to stop. Any decent human being would have. I would have. What happened after that?"

"A man stopped and asked me if I was having car troubles. I was so focused on the car seat that I didn't even hear him come up."

"Do you remember what he looked like?"

"Uhh... I'm so bad at remembering details. I don't know, similar height to me."

"Dark hair, blonde hair, any hair at all?"

"Dark, but it was dark outside too. I can't say for sure I even saw his face."

"Okay."

"It was just so—I don't even know. So weird because I remember saying to him 'there's no baby in there' and he replied 'I know.'"

Raine felt a chill up her spine. "Well, all of this is very helpful, Kevin. Thank you so much for talking with me. I'm sorry you had to go through what you did." She stood. She didn't want to take things too far and risk losing his trust. She'd already heard enough. "One more thing, Kevin. What kind of car do you drive?"

"It's a sedan. A black Toyota Camry."

Raine smiled. "All right, you take care of yourself, okay? If you remember anything, give me a call. I can leave my information with the nurses."

She left, closing the door silently behind her. Before she'd started, she'd been told the police were listening to the intercom from a room down the hall. She went there and met Detective Heely and two others, a technician and another detective

"Good work, Dr. Walsh," the technician said, and motioned her over to a chair.

She felt exhaustion settling into her limbs from the work. Since she'd had some time off, she'd forgotten how draining it was. But it was worth it.

"Raine, why ask him what car he drove?" Jonah asked.

She smiled and pulled out the chair, taking a seat. "He pulled over on the side of the road, yeah? Did you recover his car?"

Jonah sat back in the chair. "I hadn't even thought about that." He pulled out a notebook and scribbled. "That could be the piece I was missing." He pushed his chair back with a squeal. "I have to go—I'll explain later, just... I have to go." He started towards the door.

Raine got a sudden urge to confront him right now. It had to be because she'd just helped him with an important key to his case, and even though her motivation was to help the victims involved, she felt slighted.

"Excuse me, gentlemen." She nodded to the other men and took off after Jonah.

"Hey!" she called to him.

He stopped and waited. "Oh, I'm sorry, Raine! Do you have a way to get home?"

She hadn't even thought about that. Jonah brought her to the hospital. She could call Marcus. She could take public transportation, easily. "Why didn't you tell me?" she asked, tamping down her emotions.

He looked puzzled. "What? Tell you what?"

"Brandon Perez is dead."

"How the hell?"

She stood in the sterile white hallway waiting for an answer.

"It wasn't relevant to—"

"It wasn't relevant?" she repeated back to him. "Where did you find him, Jonah? Were there others? These things are important to me. Brandon... he meant a lot to me."

"There are reasons we haven't told the public, Raine."

"The public?" She held up her hand. "How am I even supposed to trust you?"

"How am I supposed to trust you, going through my files? I have to go. We'll discuss this later."

She watched him until he turned the corner, feeling as small as an ant, but still feeling the weight of Brandon's death on her shoulders.

Her phone vibrated in her purse. She waited for a moment before she pulled out the smartphone and peered at the screen.

It was a text from Arie:

"The address on the autopsy was not his family's house. It was the prison, and I'm standing outside of it."

TWELVE

Detective Heely

onah killed his engine and got out of the vehicle as a man wearing a cut off tee shirt walked towards him.

"Gus?"

"Aye," he responded, extending his hand to shake.

"I'm Jonah, we spoke on the phone."

"Come on in." He motioned to the trailer at the side of the lot. The graveled lot was full of cars with boots on their rims. He made his living towing cars parked in the wrong spots. It was a big business in San Francisco, as there were far too many no parking signs in a city with not enough spaces. Some people didn't pay attention, some would rather pay for the tow than be late to their appointments.

Jonah followed him to the trailer. When the door opened, the stench of cigarette smoke escaped. In an effort to not be rude, he restrained from lifting his sleeve to his nose.

"This will be quick. You keep—" The stench hit him like a wall when he stepped in, and he was overwhelmed for a second. He continued, "You keep records of all your pick ups?"

"Of course," Gus mumbled as he crossed to a corner desk with an ancient PC on top. He didn't reach for the keyboard. Instead he went for a binder to the left of the computer. "I got all my records right here."

"I'm interested in a particular night."

"What is it that yer lookin' for exactly?"

"Well I'm looking to see if you picked up any vehicles on a specific stretch of highway on a specific date. And it would have been at night."

Gus shoved the book toward him. "Yer welcome to poke through. I ain't got no reason to hide the information from the po-lease."

"Thank you, I appreciate it." He flipped open the book and found the date he needed. The papers were shoved carelessly in plastic sleeves. "You really make this many stops a night?"

Gus nodded. "It's good business."

"Do you remember picking up a Toyota Camry on this night? I've got the license plate number here in my phone." He reached into his pocket to retrieve the phone.

Gus leaned over him, looking into the binder to try and recall the night on the sheet. He stood a little too close to Jonah, in his comfort zone.

"Nope—no Camry."

Jonah flipped to the next car. Then the next. He'd have to follow every single one of these leads to rule them out; there was just no other way around it.

"Were all of these vehicles called in?" Jonah asked.

"Most, some by police, some by business owners. I've even had the car owners call in and ask for a tow because their car conked."

"Hm...." He was running out of options.

"There was somethin' weird about that one."

Jonah lifted his hands off the book as Gus looked down on it. "Weird?"

"That one was a customer call in. Said their tire blew."

"Okay, what's weird about that?"

"Well the owner was gone when I got there, said they'd had someone pick them up. I just towed it to their residence. Happens all the time. But when I picked up the car, this one was weird. The tire seemed like it hadn't gotten flat naturally."

"Okay, now we're getting somewhere. What did it look like, Gus?"

"Looked like someone slashed it. With a screwdriver or something."

"A screwdriver?" Jonah racked his brain. Slashed their tire on purpose? Why would someone do that? Kevin the victim's car was missing. Maybe the killer took Kevin's car and left his own? Was that a stretch? Slashed it with a screwdriver. The killer slashed his victims... with a knife. A knife!

"Gus, do you think the tire could have possibly been slashed with a knife?"

Gus scratched his chin. "Could be."

"What did you do with that car?"

"I towed it to the residence. They paid me."

"What residence? Who paid you?" He was starting to get excited. He needed to calm himself. Yes, he'd check into all the leads in that binder, but this was the closest he'd been to something tangible on this case, apart from the survivor.

"I got yer address right here." He pulled a piece of notebook paper out of a college ruled notebook next to the binder and scrawled the address from the binder onto the paper.

Jonah reached for it. "Gus, I owe you a drink sometime."

"Jus' keep bringing me business through your friends at the police station and we're even. I hope you find yer guy."

He nodded. "Thank you. I may contact you again for the rest of those tows. This is a great start but I'd like to look into everything, if you don't mind."

"Do whatcha gotta do," he said agreeably.

Jonah pocketed the piece of paper and headed for the door. "Thanks again, man!" He opened the door of the trailer and plunged into the fresh atmosphere outside. His skin, hair, and clothing felt permeated with the stench of the cigarette smoky, fogged trailer. He headed for his car. Regardless of whether this lead panned out, it was definitely a place to start.

He hopped into his car and pulled out his phone to input the address into his maps. He had several missed calls and text messages.

Surprisingly, some from Benjamin. He opened the message, and was immediately drawn away from the urgency of the case. He'd been lonely. He hadn't gone back to the apartment since that night.

The first text message said, "Let's talk. I miss you." What was he supposed to do? He loved the man. But he couldn't allow him to keep lying and cheating on him. He wanted to settle down, but Raine was right. He needed to find someone that was as passionate about their career as he was about his, that way they'd understand why he was so dedicated. Or maybe he was just supposed to be single forever. Maybe he wasn't cut out for this relationship thing.

What he *was* cut out for was detective work. Solving cases. He was feeling more down in the dumps about his cases than normal. Nothing was moving fast enough for him. However, this lead was bigger than any of the others he'd had so far. And he needed to check into all the cars in Gus's book. Starting with the car whose tire was 'slashed.' But from the description it wasn't the victim's car. And why would its owner call for a tow? It just didn't make sense.

Regardless, he needed to pay that guy a visit.

THIRTEEN

Vinnie

It was the sinking feeling of dread when he woke up and had to get ready for work that weighed him into the bed. That all too familiar feeling. Overworked and underpaid, the pressure of working in customer service. He had no choice. He had to make money so he and his wife could pay their bills and afford food. But there was something different about today. Today he had an important job to do. And it wasn't renewing car registrations and collecting people's taxes. It was much more important than that.

It was an urge that he needed to fulfill. He'd seen the lottery numbers on the news the day before while his wife was in the shower. He'd memorized the numbers. He played them over and over in his head. And work was important today because it was his job to find the license plate that matched those numbers.

The next victim.

He shut his eyes for a moment before opening them again under the florescent lights of the Department of Motor Vehicles. His eye had already begun to twitch, and he restrained himself from reaching up and holding his eyelid.

He kept telling himself he was the only one who noticed it, that nobody else could tell. Once he lifted the "next window please" sign, he'd be helping customers one after the other until he clocked out. He'd be lucky to get a break.

Maybe it would be an easy day, one where he just clicked driver's license photos and printed off the card. But no. Today it was registration and titles. He'd be turning people down all day for not having the right paperwork. People would be yelling in his face, and he'd just go about his day, as though he was numb to the interaction.

He *was* numb to most interactions. And there would only be a few moments between customers when he'd be able to dedicate his time to the hunt. The hunt to fulfill his urge.

The numbers played over and over in his head. They played on a loop while he lay in bed. They danced across his morning coffee. They appeared on every billboard as he drove to work. He didn't need to write them down. The numbers were etched in his mind like a tombstone's epitaph.

He signed into his computer database and began to type the numbers.

There was a tap on the side of his station. "You gonna help, Vin?" his coworker spat.

He looked up at her. He didn't answer. He squeezed his eyes shut again and looked up at the line. "Next," he droned.

He sent the old lady away for not having a bill that showed her address, and explained that she could renew her registration online. She asked him to repeat how she could do that. He did. She still didn't get it. He told her he needed to help the next person in line. The old lady hunched over in her wind suit, picked up her billfold and scooted to the door, an angry scowl on her face.

By the time he finished today, he'd have a matching scowl. His only solace was plugging those lottery numbers into the registry, and finding the closest combination living in the vicinity. It took more than a few tries, but he ended up nailing a name, address, and license plate.

It was a start.

He couldn't use the government computer for further details, but he was content with a name and vehicle.

It was easier to find the man than he expected. It was as simple as pulling up social media on his phone during the short break he got. The winner was a sports nut. He frequently tailgated at professional football games with his big pickup truck, beer, and grill, hours before the game started. He was a type. The guy was predictable, which made Vinnie's job tracking him down a whole lot easier. He never enjoyed the chase.

He closed the app, went into his settings, and deleted his browsing history. He didn't want any trace of this man to lead back to him. If there was one thing he'd learned about going out of his normal routine because of urges he couldn't control, it was that he needed to pay better attention to details and cover his tracks. His last blackout was messy. Too messy. Any more of those and he'd be in trouble.

He lifted the phone to his ear and listened to the ring.

"Hello?" she answered frantically with a screaming baby in the background. Scarlett was so fussy lately.

"Hey, I don't have long."

"Oh hi, Vin. How's work?"

"The same as usual. I wanted to call you and see if we had any plans on Sunday?"

"We could go to my Mother's for lunch on Saturday if it's more convenient. Why? What do you have going on?"

"Well," he hesitated. He should have come up with a better story. "Some of the guys at work want to go to the game."

"The game?"

"Yeah, the football game."

"Oh! Okay, Uh yeah, yeah we could swing that." She seemed almost too overjoyed at hearing this.

He heard the quiver in her voice, as if she didn't know what to think. It only made him feel good because that proved to him that she thought it was real. She believed his story. Of course, she always had.

"I gotta go—"

"Oh, real quick, Janet wants to know if we know whose car is parked outside their house? Probably one of the neighbor's drunk friends. She says if it's still there this afternoon they're calling a tow truck."

He swallowed nervously. "No. Didn't even notice it. Punk kids."

"Yeah, okay, I'll tell her to go right ahead."

"Okay. See you tonight."

FOURTEEN

Raine

When she saw the coffee shop, she quickened her pace. The last time she'd been there was with her friend, Melita. That seemed like ages ago. Centuries. In reality, it hadn't even been a year since she visited with her friend. They'd talked about boys and relationships, something that seemed insignificant now. It was the last thing on her mind. She was grateful for Marcus and the relationship they were in, but she couldn't even fathom it being more than it was now. Sure, she wanted to have intimacy with someone again in the future, but the memories of her past were still too much in the forefront. As long as the Warden was somewhere out there, she wasn't safe. Whether Megan was locked up or not.

She opened the shop door and the bell chimed. It startled her; she looked up at the sound before coming in, hoping nobody noticed. The only one looking at her was at a table in the back.

The boy sat with his chin propped up on a fist, his eyes glazed. He sat up straight when she caught his eye.

She hurried over, her heart beating fast. "How did you find—?"

"The address was on the autopsy report." He'd repeated what he told
her in the text message.

The sentence registered in her mind. They found Brandon's
body at the prison. He never left. She wondered what could possibly have happened. Perhaps he helped in the mutiny.

"He never left," she whispered.

"We have to go there now."

"How will we get inside?" she asked.

"I know there's a housekeeping closet on the fourth floor. If we can climb up to that window, we can get inside there and use the stairwell the rest of the way."

"You remember that?" A pang hit her stomach. *How could he possibly know that?* Though it was hard for her to fathom, a part of her mind was screaming not to trust him.

There was a pregnant pause between them.

When he spoke again, his voice was weak and it cracked. "The days after you escaped were hell, Raine. He told everyone you were dead."

She stiffened. He'd never talked about it before. She never thought to ask. She held her breath as she listened.

"I didn't believe him. I believed you had escaped. He started packing everything up. Brandon led the mutiny. He told all of us that he was going to unlock our cages and give the Warden hell, and we should help, to honor your memory. What made me think that you had survived was that the Warden and the guards began to deconstruct parts of the prison. Cages were taken down, walls stripped. At one point he even put several of us in one cage. That was fun." The last sentence dripped with sarcasm. "At the time, I didn't know Megan was who she was. She was gone though, not around. And I thought maybe she had paid for what happened as well. When he came around and issued everyone the drugs that we were supposed to take when we went out to the yard; I knew it was my only chance. Of course I had to take the drugs first. So I knew it was only a matter of time before my brain got all foggy. Several people in the cage attacked him, but I ran for it. I got as far down as the housekeeping closet, and then I started to lose control. I could only remember wandering into the lobby. I think the people in the apartment building got me to the hospital; I don't even remember that part. But I have no idea what happened to the Warden, and I didn't know that Brandon was... until you sent that text."

She sat there in shock. She hadn't prepared herself for that explanation. But it killed any suspicion, and she punished herself inside for even thinking he'd lie to her about this. She had no reason not to trust him.

He broke her train of thought, "You ready?"

"Um—" She suddenly became aware of everything in the coffee shop. Every customer. Every barista. The light music in the background, clattering dishes, and people laughing in each other's company. She pointed to the back of the shop. "I'm gonna go to the bathroom. I'll be right back." Before he could respond, she bolted, remembering from last time where the one-person bathroom was.

She went in and closed the door, locking it from the inside. Pressing herself against the door, she slid down to the floor, and allowed her emotions to overflow. With her shoulders hunched and her face in her hands, she wept. Her face was a blubbery mess, but she didn't care. In the present moment, she was safe in this tiny room.

She cried for the man that helped her escape a terrible fate. Cried for his wife and daughter, and wondered if they even knew his body had been found. Cried that she wasn't able to save him, despite the fact that he helped her so much. He believed in her and she failed him. She failed them all.

She knew she couldn't stay in that bathroom forever, and Arie was waiting.

She couldn't believe law enforcement was able to keep this covered up. And she couldn't imagine why the Warden left Brandon's body behind at the prison if he'd packed up and left. The thought crossed her mind that perhaps they hadn't. Maybe he'd thrown Brandon's body overboard, or Brandon jumped too, only he wasn't so lucky. Maybe the police didn't have to go inside at all, and the whole prison remained intact. Of course that didn't make sense, but why not? They didn't find her there. They found her in the land-fill. They thought she'd made the whole story up. What if they never looked into all the skyscrapers in the city like they said they had? The thought made her whole body tense from adrenaline.

Raine took a deep breath and stood up. She placed her hands on the sides of the sink and leaned close to the mirror. She sniffled and steeled herself.

Enough. Someone tried the knob on the bathroom door, nearly making her jump out of her skin.

Though she knew it was obvious to the person waiting that someone was in there, she felt paranoia creeping up. It was as if the person was leaning on the door, listening to every drop in the water bowl. She turned on the faucet and let the cool water flow over her hands, then splashed it on her face. The water streamed down her cheeks and she caught it with a paper towel before dripped on her shirt.

The paper towel was rough, so she dabbed her face until it was dry. Then she wadded it up and threw it away. How much time she'd spent in there started to worry her.

Why do I care so much what other people are thinking? Is it because I understand how it feels to need the already oc-cupied bathroom, or because I'm always thinking of others' comfort? She pushed open the door cautiously, half expect-ing someone to be standing there, but the little hallway was clear. They must have left after they tried the door.

As she headed back to the table, she saw nothing but two lonely mugs. She looked around the shop, although she didn't need to look because she already knew.

He was gone.

Without a second thought, she weaved through the cafe and out the bell-jingling door to the walk. She searched both sides of the street, trying get a glimpse of him.

Then her eyes landed on something else.

She saw the green dumpster and froze, and then she saw the small floral shop next door. *That's why he had me meet him here. It was so close the whole time!*

She retied her knee length, tan peacoat around her waist. Then a woman walked by briskly. The woman was looking down at her phone as she crossed at the corner and headed for an apartment building.

She's not even paying attention! Raine couldn't help but think of all the safety precautions this woman was ignoring as she walked down the street. It didn't matter that it was broad daylight. And even though she had learned a lot from her experiences, it didn't make her any more paranoid, she'd just grown in the sense that she didn't allow her paranoia to control her life. But she still carried a keychain shaped like a cat on her key ring. The cat was designed to put your fingers in the eyeholes and the ears were sharp, for defense against attackers.

However, the fact that this woman wasn't paying attention was a benefit to Raine. It gave her the chance to slip up behind her. She felt like she blended in, in her tan peacoat and skinny ankle pants. She only had one thing on her mind. She needed to get into the building and she didn't have the passcode. The woman entered her code into the keypad with Raine close behind. As the woman swung the door open, Raine leaned forward. "Oops, lemme get that for you." She smiled using her teeth, and held the door open.

The woman looked up from her phone for the first time and nodded at Raine.

"It's a beautiful day out today," she added for good measure. Small talk, something people do right?

"Sure is," the woman responded, and then turned right for the first hallway.

Raine nodded to the woman at the lobby desk and headed for the elevator. Her stomach dropped when she saw you needed a key to open it.

Jeez, the security on this building! It's no wonder nobody knew about the prison in the penthouse. She tried to remind herself that the security wasn't so good if she was able to just walk right in behind that woman. Regardless, she wouldn't be able to use the elevator, and she'd been standing in the hall long enough for the lobby receptionist to notice. She spun around. "Hi there," she said sweetly, walking to the desk. "I was wondering... Did a man come through here? He's about mid twenties, average height, skinny, light brown hair. It couldn't have been more than a few minutes or so."

The woman looked puzzled, and shook her head. "No, I don't think so. That doesn't ring a bell."

"Okay, thanks."

She considered that for a moment.

Arie never came through this lobby. He either wasn't here, or he got in some other way. *But he had to be here!* He must have had a different way in. Realizing she probably looked ridiculous trapped inside her own mind, she turned to leave. "I—I actually forgot something in my car. I'll be right back."

The woman nodded.

She headed back out the door. She'd never see that woman again anyway.

Raine rounded the corner of the building, paying attention to her peripheral vision. She looked around the alley for any signs of an entrance, and her eyes fell on the tall green dumpster butted up against the brick building next door.

That green dumpster.

Memories flooded through her like poisonous gas and she felt dizzy, enough to put her hand out to catch herself. This was the place.

She noticed her muscles were shaky and weak. She did NOT want to go back in that building.

But Arie went back in there. She had no choice.

There was a fire escape not too far up. She ran up to it and leaped with her arm outstretched. It was just a little bit out of her reach. She went to the dumpster. On her tiptoes, she peered over the edge, the sickly smell of rotting garbage overwhelming her.

What is in here that I could use? She only needed a little bit of a boost to reach the ladder. If only Arie had waited, he could have hoisted her up. Why was he in such a hurry? A pang of distrust entered her mind again and she punished herself for it. *What the hell, Raine?* She backed away from the dumpster and reached into her back pocket. Her phone. She unlocked the phone and scrolled through her contacts, landing on Arie. She hit dial.

It rang.

And rang.

No answer.

"Seriously?" she huffed. *He has to have his phone on him!*

She shoved the phone back in her pocket and walked back to the dumpster. Bags of trash full of rotting flower stems and paper waste from the flower shop next door.

Just when she was about to try to find a different entrance, the push broom caught her eye. It was jammed in with the bags of trash. The bristles were worn and smashed, but she didn't need it for its bristles. She stretched and reached as far as she could—the side of the bin cutting into her arm-pit—and she pulled out the broom.

She flipped it around so the broom was facing up. She carefully checked the street; nobody was paying any attention to the alley. She reached up with the broom, hooked the brush around the rung, then pulled it towards her.

Bingo!

The ladder slid down and she grabbed it as soon as she could reach, using her upper body strength to pull herself up. She reached out for each rung and pulled herself onto the ladder, then scooted up to the landing and crouched down while she caught her breath.

The experience reminded her of gym class back when she was in high school. They had these standardized tests for all high school students across the district, with different physical challenges. The rope was one of them. A thick, coarse rope that hung from the gym rafters all the way to the floor. Each girl had to try to climb the rope.

She looked down at her hands, her palms white from the pressure on the rungs and remembered the rope cutting into her hands. You were laughed at if you didn't get at least halfway. The pressure was motivation enough to keep climbing. She remembered thinking how stupid it was, like most subjects back in school. 'How am I going to ever use this in the real world?'

She laughed at the thought as she looked back down to the ground, where she'd just used that skill in the real world.

But there was no more time to waste. She looked up at the climb. Floors and floors of stairs. She started up, looking down at her footing through the holes in the stairs. Between each step was a view to the pavement below, should she miss her footing.

She also peered into the windows as she passed the landings, each one differently dressed. Some of them were completely open into the lofts and apartments. She couldn't fathom why they were okay with having their privacy completely exposed, except that people don't frequent the fire escapes.

She reached the end; there were no more stairs. She looked up at the building, it went much higher than where she stood.

What do all the people on those floors do in the case of a fire? she wondered, before the answer flashed in her mind. *They jump.* She remembered the adrenaline and pain throughout her body the last time she was here.

She turned to face the window of this last platform, and her eyes instantly caught the hairline crack in the glass. She followed it down to the bottom windowpane, which was completely smashed out.

Arie.

He was here. He broke that window.

She knelt down, squinting inside. The room was dark, but she could tell it was small. She squeezed through the broken window feet first. When she landed and her eyes adjusted to the light, she took in her surroundings. She was inside a housekeeper's closet, probably the custodian of the apartment building. Arie knew exactly where this was. She'd find him.

She dodged the yellow mop buckets and brooms to the door. Propping it open, she peeked out the door and looked both ways down the hallway. The coast was clear. The walls were beige and the floor was a deep mahogany wood, with modern light fixtures in the ceiling. There were numbered doors, but it was apparently unoccupied. She slipped out of the closet and walked with purpose to the door at the end of the hall. She pushed it open and stumbled into the stairwell. This one was a little less scary than the fire escape until the door slammed behind her. Her heart began to pound because she knew what was at the top. She pushed forward anyway.

Her feet were bags of sand, heavier with each step. The higher she climbed, the higher her anxiety level rose. She pulled her smartphone from her pocket and squeezed it until her knuckles turned white. Judging by her experience in the car not too long ago, this phone was a false sense of security. She knew that, but it comforted her nonetheless. The fact that someone, anyone, could be at the other end of that line should she need them. It also provided a flashlight in the dim stairwell.

The stairwell was a reminder of a place she never wanted to visit again. An experience that haunted her. Escaping the prison was a monumental accomplishment that put many challenges in her life in perspective. She was able to see past her paranoia and anxiety from the things that happened in her life before her kidnapping. Escaping the prison and fighting for her life was a healing moment for her. She realized she could take back her life.

Yes, it did that for her. But it did the opposite as well. The fact that she had no solid conclusion. The fact that the Warden was still out there. The fact that the police were moving on to other cases, and distracting her from her own by making her focus on another, as if hers didn't matter anymore. She wasn't fighting that because she needed closure, though she did, she was fighting it because there were others involved that were still imprisoned. They had gone missing just like she had. They also had families. They helped her escape. And she thought that by taking the risk and jumping, she would be helping them. And just knowing that only she and Arie had escaped made her feel guilty, and weighed her down to the point where she couldn't move on with her life. She needed to move on desperately, and she just couldn't. So naturally, being back in this stairwell, taking each step as quickly as it came, closer and closer to a place she never wanted to be again, had to happen.

The image she held of Arie, this boy who emotionally and mentally guided her through the prison—was misleading. He was fighting his own battles. Arie was an internalizer. It was obvious he didn't share all his demons with her. Maybe they could help each other if he wasn't. But perhaps she was so closely part of his experience that she couldn't help him either. Generally, she was able to separate personal from business, but in this case, they came together. She just couldn't separate them.

She passed doors but she had to continue going all the way to the top. She wasn't sure what was on the other side, and memories of the different rooms she'd been in came to her. She couldn't piece together a floor plan because it was such a maze, and when she was here she was so disoriented that she wasn't sure if what she saw was real or not. Disorientation was powerful. And it worked. She couldn't picture where the loft was in reference to the cages. Or the guard's quarters. Or the intake room. It was all a blur.

So she continued going up until the stairs ended. Her breath echoed in the empty stairwell, loud, exasperated, and short. Wheezing slightly from exertion.

No more time to waste. She pushed through the door.

Darkness.

She stood in the stairwell with the door open, struggling to hold the heavy door open. The first thing that was clear was the complete darkness. There were no lights. She glanced back at the stairwell. The dark oblivion ahead of her was almost a symbol of the unknown. She was unsure what she was going into, unsure of the goal, and unsure of what she would encounter.

Once again it was her only option. She came all the way up here. She cursed to herself, too afraid to call into the dark for Arie, for fear of what else might answer. She thought about the fact that she had no way to defend herself.

How could I be so stupid! she thought. She didn't even have her keys. Originally she'd expected to use the buddy system, teamed up with Arie. She had a quick burst of anger at him for not waiting, if he was in here at all. And she directed that same anger at herself for shutting off her common sense. She didn't tell Marcus or anyone else that she was coming here. He would be so angry with her for taking the risk. For playing a dangerous game, which was exactly what she was doing. Isolation seeped into her bones, like the last time she was here.

She tapped her phone, brought up the flashlight and entered. The quiet click of the latch reuniting with the doorframe sounded like a slam when it echoed. Shaking, she held her phone flashlight up and tried to see as much as she could. It was a hallway, as expected. She stood with her back against the cool concrete wall, her ears pricked in the echoing silence.

Nothing.

She worked up the nerve to walk down the hall. She ran her hand along the wall, high above her head. Her fingers touched dips in the concrete, the two holes the size of small screws. A wall sconce used to be there. Those caged Edison bulb lights. It'd been removed. And judging by the darkness of the hallway, all the lights, light bulbs, and the entire sconces were gone. From memory, she knew there had to be a set of double doors coming up on the right hand side soon.

Sure enough, as she scanned down the wall with the flashlight pointed ahead and down, her hand brushed the hinge of the first door. She turned the knob and pushed it open, the screech loud in her ears, bringing an avalanche of memories crashing down at once. She slipped and crouched, the phone dropping from her hands to the floor.

The moment it hit, the light went out.

She covered her ears, shut her eyes tight, and trembled.

Shit, shit, shit, she repeated over and over in her mind, regretting everything. Regretting coming here. She needed to move.

Get it together, Raine!

She reached around for her phone. When she found it, she scooped it up and hit the home button. The screen lit up, revealing a spider web of cracks. She let out an exasperated sigh. The concrete she dropped it on must have hit the screen just right, enough to shatter it. Thankfully it still worked.

She held it up and looked around. It was just a large empty room. There were no cages, no dividers, nothing. Just a large, basement-like room with high ceilings. Had the police come they wouldn't have seen anything. Arie was right. Megan was right. The police were right. The Warden cleaned out everything, and left it abandoned. With no trace that anything ever existed here to begin with.

She felt defeated. She scanned the phone across the floor, walking with hesitation. When she got to the middle of the room, so she thought, there was something that looked like a shadow on the floor. She froze.

She crouched down and held her phone over it. It was a burnt brown color.

Blood.

She covered her mouth with her hand. *What did I expect, coming here?* she screamed in her mind. Then she heard a resounding bang. She jumped from her crouch turned around.

She didn't know if she should yell, try and get their attention, let them know that she was in here, or if she should hide.

It could be Arie. But it also might not be.

She heard footsteps coming closer and closer. And then she saw the light.

"Ar—Arie?" she quavered.

He was in front of her, a few yards away. Her light reflected off of his gun.

A gun.

"Arie?" She moved her light up to his face. Tear stained and red. His eyes bloodshot.

"Why—put the gun down," she said.

He wasn't sure what he wanted to do with it. He began to raise it.

Would he shoot her? What was happening? But he didn't point it at her.

He raised the gun to his own temple.

"Please!" she shouted. "Arie, no. Put the gun down. Please. I love you."

His eyes were wide, unblinking.

"You don't need to do this. Please," she begged. "I'm coming over there."

He didn't move.

She went to him and set the phone on the floor, the light casting deep shadows on their faces.

Arie allowed her to take the gun and put it on the floor. He collapsed on her and his weight pulled her down. She managed to keep him from hitting the floor. She threw her arms around him and hugged him, his head on her shoulder. She helped him to sit on the floor, and they continued to hold each other.

She had so many questions for him. "Where did you get the gun?" she asked.

"It's a BB gun." His voice was quiet.

She nodded. "Enough to do some damage though. Why didn't you wait for me?" She wasn't sure it was smart to ask this now, but it spilled out.

"I had to see for myself."

She understood. "Arie. I understand. I feel the way you feel." They sat in silence for quite a while. "He's not here, Arie. You shouldn't have come here alone."

"We need to go back to Megan. And I need to talk to her. Not you. Me."

"She'll disappoint you, Arie. She *will* hurt you."

"She can't hurt me more than she already has."

FIFTEEN

Detective Heely

He sat low in the driver's seat, and watched. Stalked.

A blue light flickered through the front window. No doubt the source was a television. It was soothing and his eyelids grew heavy. He was far past working hours, but the work never stopped.

He perked up at the sound of a car and leaned below the window.

The car pulled into the driveway and the garage door opened.

Bingo. It was his guy.

He tried to focus on the garage, to see if he could see anything inside. A workbench, a lawn mower, a trash bin. Nothing out of the ordinary. The car pulled in and the door closed after it. He saw movement in the window, and more light flooded the TV room.

Jonah looked over at the passenger seat. There was the sheet of paper that listed the names and addresses of everyone that was towed that night. He knew that he would be checking out every name on the list. But why not start with the one that stood out to him, the one with the flat tire? What were the odds that the first person he checked out happened to be his guy?

His mind switched gears, to thinking about Raine Walsh. He'd intended to tell her, but he needed her to concentrate on the case they were working on.

She snooped on my desk. How can I trust her?

Could he blame her? Chances were if he put himself in her shoes, he'd do the same thing. And it was his fault he left the office. At least she hadn't seen the map he had in the conference room. Then he'd really be in trouble. He would speak with her soon enough and get everything straightened out.

He brought his attention back to the house. *Had it been long enough?* He wanted the man to get settled before he went up to the door and started asking questions.

Jonah maneuvered the car from its spot. He pulled up to the potential suspect's house and turned the car off, grabbed his badge and got out. He tapped his hip to be sure his gun was secure in its holster under his clothes.

There was always a burst of adrenaline when he approached the door of a cold call. He never knew what would be on the other side. When he left patrol, one of the pros was that the danger would be more predictable. On the street, things could turn in a second. Even at traffic stops, you never knew what you were getting into. And domestic violence stops were the worst. Being a detective was far less risky. Or so he thought.

He knocked three times, and then stood back. Someone shuffled inside the house, and the door swung open.

A man stood there, staring back at him. Dark hair hung below his ears. A long, narrow nose. His eyes were wary. But what surprised Jonah was the other pair of eyes staring at him.

On the man's hip was a baby girl with the same wide, periwinkle blue eyes. She sat there and smiled as she blew bubbles with her drool. The man didn't say a word.

"Uh, Mr. Wilson?" he asked, getting straight down to business.

He nodded.

"I won't take much of your time," He flipped out his badge and flashed it. The baby reached forward to grab the shiny object but the man stepped back, his face blank.

Jonah felt awkward in the silence, the fact that man wasn't reacting with words.

"I'm here about your car. You had it towed. I need to know that it's been taken care of."

"But you know that already," the man said. "Oh?" he asked.

"Well you saw me drive into my driveway. Just now." Vinnie

nodded at the street where Jonah had been parked for most of the day.

He didn't know what to say.

"Can I ask why you've been watching my house all day, Detective?"

The way he said detective, with that punch, almost as if the word was an insult, did not sit well with Jonah. It was weird. Unusual. It was clear Vinnie Wilson was socially awkward, unable to respond appropriately to people. But he also knew the exact words to say, as if he'd carefully select-ed them before he spoke.

"My tire was fixed, and my wife and I got great service from Gus. Anything else I can help you with?"

Why did I even come here? What was my purpose for coming up to this door? "No, that sounds good. I'm glad you were able to get your tire fixed. Uhh, question. How exactly was your tire cut with a knife driving down the interstate?"

Once again, Mr. Vinnie Wilson didn't react. He just looked into space over Jonah's shoulder.

"Must have run over something sharp," he mumbled.

Jonah nodded. *That was no answer.* The fact that he wouldn't get a straight answer was both troubling and good news all in one. This man definitely needed to be brought in for questioning.

"Well, I won't take any more of you and your family's time, but be careful out there. There's a killer on the loose, armed with a knife." He generally wouldn't tell a civilian this information. He wasn't entirely sure if the media was aware. They still didn't want to scare or alarm the general public until they had more information.

Vinnie nodded and reached for the door, slamming it in Jonah's face.

It wasn't the first time he had a door slammed in his face. It wouldn't be the last time either.

But he got what he came here for. He hurried back to the car and hopped in, grabbing his notebook. He detailed as much of the interaction as he could remember. Exactly as he could remember it. Every detail.

It came as a bit of a shock that the guy had a family. The baby was cute and happy. These kinds of guys usually lived alone. He was almost too obvious a choice, until Jonah saw the family.

Still, none of this explained the victim's missing car. Or any connection this case might have to the prison case.

He needed to get away from this house. Because judging by the conversation he'd just had, he was watched as much as he was watching.

And he needed sleep.

He would check out the other leads, but this meeting confirmed that from now on, he would be watching Vinnie like a hawk.

He left the neighborhood, racking his mind for a plan. *Sleep in my car again? Or go to the beach and lay out in the sand, even though the night is chilly. And the sand fleas. Scratch that idea.* He wasn't homeless.

Exactly. He wasn't homeless. He could go back to his apartment, though he ran the risk of running into Benjamin. He could kick him out. But he wasn't in the mood for talking now. He had no energy for talking. Avoidance was much easier than kicking his boyfriend out. But he let his muscle memory drive him home, thinking about the case, and what he was going to need to do next.

He parallel parked close to his apartment. Even though it was his usual spot, he still checked for signs. San Francisco parking was tricky. Recycling pick up one day, street cleaning the next. He needed to make sure his car wasn't going to be towed while he slept. He'd come out of his apartment far too many times, running late for work, only to find that he parked his car in the wrong place on the wrong day.

Speaking of tows, he would need to check out all the other leads that Gus gave. From the car to his door, he went back through the conversation he'd just had with Vinnie Wilson. The man was weird. Socially awkward and something just wasn't right with him.

His mind was buzzing. As he reached the second set of stairs, he was suddenly dizzy. He dug in his pocket for the key, but when he rattled the knob, the door swung open. It was already unlocked. *Great security there, Ben!* The painful thought of another man inside his apartment, in his bed with Ben crossed his mind. He'd been gone a few days; he wasn't sure what he was coming back to. He tossed his keys onto the kitchen counter and started to walk into the dimly lit family room. Just as he reached the couch, a shadow appeared in the doorway of the bedroom.

"Who's... who's here with you?" Jonah asked.

Benjamin shook his head. "Just me," he whispered. He hesitated a moment and then crossed the room.

Jonah collapsed onto the couch.

Benjamin crouched and began to untie Jonah's boots, flicking the laces with ease and slipping them off.

He leaned his head back when Benjamin gently rolled his knuckles in the arch of his foot. His eyes closed. Ben always knew what to do to make him feel good. Should he fight it? Should he let this guy back into his life?

He was so exhausted. It felt good. It was only a massage.

Before he knew it, Benjamin had worked his way up to his chest and began to unbutton his shirt. No speaking, just action, as if he was aware that Jonah didn't want to talk about it. As if Benjamin knew him better than he knew himself.

Benjamin slipped his hand under the shirt. He traced Jonah's nipple, then up to his neck.

"Ben..." He pushed the hand away. "I'm just..."

"Relax," Benjamin coaxed. "I'm an asshole. I shouldn't have been unfaithful to you."

Jonah shook his head. "Not now," he whispered.

"You work so hard. I was afraid you'd never come back. I'm not entirely sure I'm not dreaming now."

He couldn't stop the smile.

"Come on, Jonah, let's get you in the bath." He pulled on his arm.

Jonah obliged. He needed a shower badly. He wanted to wash the work off him. He wanted to start fresh on so many different aspects of his life. He moseyed into the bathroom, shedding clothing as he went with the help of his lover.

Jonah lay in bed.

"You love it?"

He turned his head to look at Benjamin lying next to him "Love what?"

"Your job."

He smoothed down his now clean blonde hair. It smelled of smoky Oud Wood and vanilla.

"Why else would I dedicate my life to it?"

"Why did you want to be a cop?"

"I like the challenge. I like helping people."

"Can I have the non media version?"

Jonah squeezed his eyes shut and let out an exasperated laugh. "Uhh, I dunno. Maybe I needed something I felt confident about."

"You seem like a pretty confident guy."

He laughed again. "Maybe now. But growing up? Come on. I was the fag that was picked last in gym class."

Benjamin sat up. "Yeah, it must of sucked growing up in the Midwest."

"Mm," he agreed.

"You want a drink?"

"Sure. Nothing with caffeine though," he slurred, his eyes itching with fatigue.

Benjamin leaned forward, almost hesitant, as if to ask if it was appropriate.

He felt they were past appropriate, so he offered his lips and Ben sealed the space between them. Ben's lips were full and soft and comforting on his. He felt connected to this other human in front of him, and he deeply cared for him, no matter how many times he'd been hurt.

Ben stood up, and Jonah watched him go, wearing only his gray boxer briefs.

Relaxed from the bath and enjoying the cool sheets was enough to slow his heart rate. His eyes grew heavier and heavier. He heard the faint sound of ice cubes plinking into a glass, grow fainter and fainter.

He was asleep before Benjamin returned.

SIXTEEN

Vinnie

After Scarlett fell asleep, he put her in the playpen and went to the kitchen to get dinner started. He pulled a yellow onion and a green bell pepper from the fridge. When he took a knife from the butcher block, he held it up and stared at his reflection in the blade. The handle felt com-fortable against his palm. Natural.

His wife shuffled boxes around in the family room. As he positioned the pepper on the cutting board of the kitchen island, he watched her open the boxes and take out bags of clothes. Then she ripped into the plastic bags and laid cloth-ing out on the couch.

"What the hell is all that?" he asked, slicing the pepper with the knife, so sharp that it cut like there was nothing there to resist.

"I told you the other night that I was going to be a clothing rep for this online company." She glanced at him and held up a pair of patterned leggings. "Aren't these cute?"

"Jeezuz, Gwen, how much did all that shit cost?"

She was quiet a moment, then protested, "I'm going to sell it all. I just had to pay for it up front but—"

"Gwen! We're already struggling as it is! Look at this stack of bills here!" His stomach did a sickly flip when he looked down at the knife he'd just used on the pepper. He'd gotten so upset that he failed to notice he'd sliced it right through his finger. Like it was waiting for him to notice, deep crimson blood began to run thickly from his finger. The knife slipped from his hand to the counter and he hugged his hand to his chest.

He saw blood all the time. But this was his. It was dizzying. Alarming.

Gwen leapt up from the couch and rushed to his side. She grabbed a towel from the rack and reached for his hand.

He felt stupid, and humiliated for not being careful, and here was his wife, helping him when he was just such a jerk to her. He held his hand tightly against his shirt.

"Lemme see," she coaxed him. "C'mon now." She forced his hand away from his chest and he fanned open his fingers.

The cut was on the inside of his thumb, and bad.

"It's deep, but not to the bone. I don't think you'll need stitches. Keep pressure on there a second, I'll be right back. Pay attention, huh?"

Her tone was teasing, but he didn't see any humor in the situation. It felt as though his arm was cut off. And he couldn't help but think it had something to do with karma.

Gwen came back, crinkling open a bandage. She wrapped the bandage around his thumb quite competently and secured it. "How come you didn't tell me there was a cop at our door earlier?" she asked, her voice soft and innocent.

Vinnie looked her in the eyes, and then away from her, he grabbed the pepper and ran it under cold water to buy time.

"It was nothing, and I didn't want you to worry."

"Why was he here?" she asked.

He wondered the same thing himself. It was worrisome. What was the meddling detective hiding?

"Said he was checking with everyone who used the same tow service the day I got that flat. Who knows, maybe something happened with the tow service?"

"Hmm," she responded. The answer must have been enough to satisfy her because she retreated back to the family room and began to organize the clothing again.

Why *was* that detective at their door? It couldn't have been specifically because of the tow man. Were they on to him? The paranoia was debilitating and somehow made the throbbing pain under the bandage worse.

Maybe he wasn't as careful as he thought he was? Maybe he was too careless when he skipped the routine. He regretted it. It didn't fulfill his need like the others had. And it was distracting his planning for the next one. Perhaps he needed to look into this detective like the detective was looking into him.

He finished slicing the vegetables and threw them into a hot oiled skillet. It was easy to slice some veggies and chicken and toss them in the pan until they were finished. He was able to think about his next victim's social media profile, and what a douche the guy appeared to be. Usually Vinnie didn't waste his time figuring out who the person really was. When they felt like a stranger to him, it was easier to blend in with the crowd. But he already hated this guy, because he was forcing him to go to a sporting event. The only thing that was good for him was the fact that it was such a public event. There would be thousands of people there. Thousands. More than any amount Vinnie'd ever killed in front of.

The construction site was a challenge because there were lots of people around, but he didn't get caught. The number of people at the football game was on his side. Because when there were a lot of people, the bystander effect took place. It never failed. People didn't want to be inconvenienced. And people didn't want to butt in. The human mind was an amazing thing, but it had some blind spots.

He saw the bystander effect take place while he was humiliated with the fake lottery ticket. Everyone laughed. They were happy that it wasn't them, or they believed he thought it was funny too. He didn't.

"So who are these guys you're going to the game with?" Her voice came from the other room and penetrated his thoughts as if she could hear them.

It startled him.

"Uhh, you know, just some guys over in accounting." It was the first thing he could think of. And he was grateful he'd chosen a department of people whose wives didn't talk to his wife

"Wives coming?" she asked.

He hadn't even considered she might ask. "Uh, no, I don't think so. Did you wanna come?"

She laughed. "As much fun as that sounds—a football game in the cold with the guys from accounting, I think I'll just let you go and have fun."

He smirked. The trick to keeping any woman happy was to make her think what you wanted was her idea. Worked every time.

He turned down the heat as the vegetables began to sizzle, and shook the pan back and forth. "Let's eat," he said as he reached for plates, "and you can tell me more about this clothing rep thing you're doing."

He'd have to continue plotting the football game later.

Vinnie stared at the ceiling of the bedroom. His left eye twitched. He focused on the spasms. Generally his insomnia was accompanied by a mind that couldn't settle. All the things he had to do, things he should have done that day, or should have said to a particular person. And all the specific details inside and out. But tonight was different. His mind was easy. Blank. Nothing but the twitch in his left eyelid, but that was enough. He turned onto his side, as slowly and carefully as possible, so he didn't wake up Gwen.

"Vinnie?"

Too late. She was awake. Her voice was soft and groggy.

He looked over his shoulder at her.

"Can't sleep again?" she asked.

He didn't realize she'd noticed. "I'm okay," he whispered.

She put her hand on his shoulder.

He rolled over to face her.

She was wearing one of his t-shirts, which looked big on her smaller frame.

"No. You need sleep."

He ignored her genuine look of concern.

"You're different. We've been so distant from each other. Is it because we haven't had much sex since Scarlett was born? I just haven't been feeling up to it since she was born and—"

"No, it's not that, Gwen. It's nothing. Go to sleep."

"I want to talk about this. If you're not going to go to sleep anyway, then why not talk?"

"What do you want from me?"

She pursed her lips. "I want you back."

"I don't understand what you mean."

"Vinnie... I want—Don't get mad. I want to go to a therapist with you."

He raised one eyebrow. "Therapist? Why?"

"Well I think it could really help us."

"What do we need help with? Come on, we're fine. Here—" He reached over and cupped her breast.

She pulled away from him. "No!" she whispered, most likely because she didn't want to wake the baby.

Vinnie pulled his hand back as if a snake had bitten him. "I thought you wanted *intimacy*. Thought you weren't getting enough of it."

She scrambled out of the sheets.

"Oh, come on. Now you're angry?"

She crossed her arms over her chest. "Who are you?"

He just shrugged. "I'm sorry."

She shook her head.

"What, now I can't apologize?"

"You can apologize by showing up at the therapist on Thursday." She grabbed her pillow and left him there.

"No, no, no." Now it was Vinnie's turn to scramble out of bed. "You stay here. I'll go. I'm not sleeping anyway."

She put her chin down and went back to the bed.

Before he left he asked, "Thursday?"

She nodded.

"Okay, Thursday. I love you, Gwen. Goodnight.

"'Night," she sniffled.

Then he shut the door behind him, and cursed himself on the way to the family room.

SEVENTEEN

Raine

Raine took a sip of her warm tropical green tea and set it back down on her desk. She clicked through files, still getting used to the new electronic filing system. Leaning over, she grabbed some papers off the printer, enjoying the warmth of the freshly printed page.

Fresh, clean, intake forms meant that she'd be seeing clients. It'd been so long, too long since she'd seen any clients. She missed it. Her own therapist didn't think it was a good idea. Sure, she could go to work because it was a great distraction, and doing familiar things would help her gain back a sense of normalcy. But she wasn't seeing clients. She missed the energy she got when she helped others. And Marcus was beginning to feel overwhelmed by his workload.

There was a knock at her door. "Yes?" she called out.

Marcus stuck his smiling face in. "You need anything?" he asked.

She shook her head. "Naw, thank you though. My three o'clock should be here soon." She loved the way it sounded on her lips. So natural. She had a purpose.

"Are you ready?" he asked.

"Don't make it weird now." She hid her smile.

"Well, it's been a while. I want to make sure we're not throwing you back to the dogs too fast."

That expression made her think of Arie and her smile faded. "I'm okay." She looked back at the computer, away from the question on his face. *Arie.* She hoped he was okay now. It had taken her some time to calm him before they made their way back down the skyscraper. She remembered the face of the woman behind the front desk when they passed. She had a look of confusion when she saw Raine with the man that she had asked about no more than an hour before.

But Raine didn't care. She was walking out of that building with Arie alive. Again. And she'd likely never see that woman behind the desk after this. Her eyes flicked up to Marcus. "I'll let you know if I need anything. Do *you* need anything?"

"Classic therapist move."

"Huh?"

"Deflecting. You have a natural talent."

"Thank you." She rolled her eyes.

"Dr. Altor?" Sylvie called from the other room.

"My next appointment is here. We'll talk in a bit, yeah?" he asked.

She nodded, smiling at him.

After Marcus left, Raine felt guilty she hadn't told him about her field trip with Arie to the skyscraper. She wasn't sure why telling him was so hard, because she should feel like she could share anything with him. Maybe the fact that she hadn't gotten an intimate chance to bring it up was a factor. Or how aggressively he'd been overprotecting her lately. He didn't understand that she needed to bring closure to her nightmare. He probably thought that authorities could take care of it, but it was clear that they couldn't.

She shook the thought from her mind.

I need to focus on my appointment. She lit incense. Scent was still an important part of her practice, even after its role in her nightmare. She chose a bright, inviting scent, Sweet Orange. The citrus was for uplifting and energizing.

She didn't generally meet with couples. But Marcus was falling behind and she decided to take the family on.

She picked up a tie and pulled her hair into a twist on her head, securing the bun with the tie. She checked the time and then slid her phone into her desk drawer. She didn't like to have it during sessions. A phone was a distraction. She hated nothing more than someone poking at their phone while she was trying to have a conversation with them. Speaking to people, knowing their minds were elsewhere, was frustrating.

She opened her door, motioning to Sylvie that she was ready.

"Hi there!" she smiled at the couple.

The woman was blond and pretty, with high cheekbones and a clean, natural face. "Hello, Dr. Walsh. I'm Gweneth Wilson." She sounded eager.

Raine shook hands with her, then motioned them to the sofa.

"This is my husband, Vinnie."

Raine offered her hand to Vinnie and noticed the bandage on his thumb. She felt his reluctance as she shook his hand.

She saw this dynamic all the time in the waiting room. The woman usually convinced the man that they needed therapy, or that the only way she could be happy was through counseling. And the man was usually reluctant and in denial about whether therapy could work for them. It most definitely wasn't like that for all couples, but she felt that energy right away with the Wilsons.

"So today is going to be just sort of an intake session. We aren't going to get deep into anything, but I'd like to just talk with you two collectively, you know, about what brought you here and then we'll schedule break out sessions where I'd like to speak with each of you individually before we can develop an action plan. How does that sound?"

Gwen nodded her head.

Vinnie turned his head away for a moment, rubbing at his temple before coming back to the conversation. He leaned forward on the sofa and stared at the ground.

Raine observed their body language. All of this was important in helping them. "So what brings you guys here today?"

Vinnie continued to look at the floor, but it wasn't necessary for him to talk because Gwen spoke right up. "I feel like my husband and I have been growing apart since the birth of our baby girl." She touched her hair a lot, and tapped her foot. "I just need… an unbiased opinion, and I thought I'd come by myself, but I want Vinnie to talk stuff out too. He's been so distant."

He didn't say anything, but Raine caught the look of distaste directed at his wife. She also observed Gwen's reaction to that. That is why the separate sessions were so important. You can't always say things in front of your spouse, there was much more insight to be had visiting with them individually. Sometimes the client wasn't worried about the possibility of hurting their partner. When they were at the point where hurting the other wasn't a concern, things were bad. This couple was not to that point. They were still in the stage where the wife was afraid to share how she felt.

"Well we can talk about that, and find the reasons for these feelings. But you being here now is an important first step. Mental health is important to address, just like you'd go to the hairdresser or to the gym. Even if you feel nervous about being here or maybe you feel like you don't even belong here, everyone can benefit from speaking to a therapist."

"Of course you'd say that," Vinnie mumbled.

"Excuse me?" Raine asked, maintaining her professionalism.

"Of course you'd say everyone can benefit and that you should visit a therapist regularly—you're a therapist." His tone was dry.

"Vin!"

"It's all right." Raine held her hand up, watching him. "All I ask is that you keep an open mind, Vinnie. You're here for a reason. Even if that reason is to appease your wife, you still have a choice. I appreciate you being here."

"I appreciate you being here too," Gwen said with a soft voice.

"Where did you get your credentials, Dr. Walsh?" Vinnie asked.

The question came as a surprise to her, because clients didn't generally ask her questions about her life right away. Unless of course they were deflecting, which happened sometimes. And she was very careful not to share personal information, so a client couldn't use it to manipulate her in any way. Most of the time it was only the seriously disturbed clients that tried to latch onto her personal life. Though a question like where she got her credentials was not an inappropriate one, especially at the first meeting.

"Seriously, Vinnie. She was very highly recommended." Gwen seemed annoyed, rolling her eyes in the direction of her husband.

Raine pointed to the bookshelves where she displayed her diploma. "I received my PhD at the Department of Psychology at Stanford University. I've been in clinical psychology at this office for several years now."

They didn't need to know about her sabbatical, something that was still fresh. Something that was always at the back of her mind, as if each client could smell it on her. She stuffed that insecurity back into a deep, dark place in her mind.

"I thought I recognized you," he smirked.

"Oh! Vinnie went to Stanford too." Gwen said happily.

"Did you?" she asked, racking her brain for any memory of his face. She hadn't recognized him at all. He seemed a little older than she was. "What were you studying?"

"Marketing. But I took quite a few psychology classes as well. You were much younger but I think you were in one of my classes."

"What year did you graduate?"

"I didn't."

She pulled back. That might be something he was sensitive about. Something he felt was holding him back. She turned the therapist back on. "There's nothing wrong with that. Sometimes life pulls us in a different direction."

"Yeah," he said with amusement. "Very different directions."

She wasn't sure what he was implying, and she couldn't tell if she was detecting sarcasm or not because she didn't know him well.

"I thought that having Scarlett would be the best thing that could happen to us." Gwen hung her head. "This is *not* about the baby, Gwen!" He raised his voice for the first time in the session.

Short tempered. She wished she had her notebook close, but this was only the intake session. She didn't want to make them nervous by taking notes, which made so many people uncomfortable. The thought of someone else judging you never sat well with anyone, even if they knew you were trying to help them.

She waited for one of them to continue but Gwen gave Raine a helpless look.

"Vinnie, maybe you could put yourself in your wife's shoes for a moment here. You may not think the baby is the reason for the way you feel right now, but Gwen does. Why do you think she feels that way? We need to figure out why Gwen is having those feelings. You are each experiencing feelings that the other might not understand. You might not understand them yourself. And that's all right. We can work this out, okay?"

"Thank you, Dr. Walsh." Gwen mumbled.

"Lets go ahead and schedule your individual sessions with Sylvie before you leave today. I just want to ask, is there anything you'd like to share with me before we get started?" Raine asked.

Vinnie looked down, and Gwen shook her head. "We're just happy you were able to meet with us, I've called a few times but you've been booked up."

She was thankful for Sylvie, who saved face for her and kept her life private, as she should. This woman in front of her thought she was booked up with clients, when in reality she was working through therapy herself.

Helping Detective Heely with the Bystander Killer case was the best thing for her. This entire time she'd been caught up in her own wants, her own case, and her own conclusion. How selfish could she be? Did an offhand remark from her first client break the spell? She needed to help Heely and the authorities catch a person brutally stabbing others to death. Anyone could be next as long as the killer was on the loose. Even though she was upset with Heely for holding so much back, she needed to help Kevin and these victims.

Because of that moment, she was happy to have taken a chance to get back into the swing of seeing clients. Even though it had its challenges, it was where she was meant to be.

EIGHTEEN

Detective Heely

J onah cut the engine and sat in the car, looking up at
the weathered strip mall. A frazzled woman walked into
the building, a manila folder tucked under her arm. He
glanced at the scribbles on the legal pad on the seat next to
him. He pulled open the glove compartment, and retrieved
his car insurance and registration. He picked up the pad and
attempted to decipher his chicken scratches. He hardly remembered the map he sketched the previous night.

He had a relaxing and welcoming evening with
Benjamin, and he barely remembered falling asleep. But he
woke with the moon still high in the sky, and couldn't get
back to sleep. He wished for just one full night of sleep.
Even just a few hours of rest. His mind was always active,
always working, always hammering out details his subcon-
scious caught that hadn't surfaced yet.

What was the next step with Mr. Wilson? He'd gotten a
chance to check out some of the other leads: a businessman,
excited to use the spray can of tire inflator and sealer, and
wouldn't shut up about the fact that new cars didn't come
with a spare tire anymore. The rest offered just as little. But

Mr. Wilson. Vinnie Wilson. Sure he was socially awkward, but could he be a murderer?

He thought about the baby. But just because the guy held a baby didn't mean he wasn't capable of taking the lives of innocent people. Did he have a history of mental illness? Would he allow the detective to search his house? These were all points written on the legal pad. Questions that would keep him up all hours of the night until he could answer them.

After he finished renewing registration on his car, he'd take another trip over to the Wilsons house. Maybe he could catch his wife before Vinnie got home. Maybe she'd even let him inside to have a look around. It was worth a shot.

Jonah got out of the car and headed into the dreaded Department of Motor Vehicles.

He took a number from the machine and went for the uncomfortable plastic chairs. His temples were already throbbing. The florescent lights did it every time. Luckily he didn't have to go to the DMV often, because it took the entire year to muster the patience to do it again. He had to sit next to a woman with a screaming baby. That didn't help.

He shut it out to the best of his abilities until his number was called. *I hope I have all my damn papers,* he thought. Why didn't he check before he was called?

He stepped up to the cubicle and set his information on the counter. Then he looked at the window's occupant, directly into the icy, emotionless blue eyes.

What?

"Excuse me, sir. If you're not ready then you'll need to step aside." His voice was low, emotionless, bored, drained.

Sir? Did he recognize me? "Registration," he coughed to clear his throat.

Vinnie reached across the counter and pulled the paperwork over, not concealing his smirk.

Was Jonah imagining it? *No.* He knew who Jonah was. And now he was going to toy with him.

"Do you need new plates?"

Jonah had tuned out, hearing the sentence as if it was down a tunnel. He was looking past Vinnie's shoulder at the stack of license plates on the counter behind him. Shiny and new.

License plates.

This guy had access to license plates. *Did he take some home?* This was one of the most puzzling things about the Bystander Killer crimes. The vehicles that disappeared. They still hadn't recovered Kevin's vehicle. And that story didn't add up. Besides sinking the cars into a body of water, which would be hard to hide, how else could a guy make a vehicle invisible? Give it a new identity.

A new license plate.

The murderer was standing right in front of him, on the other side of the counter. Of course this was all speculation. Of course he didn't have any probable cause to arrest the guy. He needed something bigger.

"What happened to your thumb?"

"Wouldn't you like to know, *Detective?*" He emphasized the last word. "I know you've been watching."

Jonah raised an eyebrow.

"I've been watching *you* too."

The warning was enough to do the trick. Enough for him to convince himself that this was his guy, and he vowed right then and there that he would *not* get away with it.

Jonah put his cash on the counter. The exact amount. "I won't stop."

"I don't know what you're talking about. You will receive confirmation in the mail within two weeks. Next!" He hit the button that called the next number.

"I won't stop until you've endured more than that thumb injury."

"Good day, Detective."

His smirk was the last thing Jonah saw as he left the DMV. He got him. He got him! Now all he had to do was prove it.

NINETEEN

Raine

The drive was one she'd been used to, one that she had taken so many times since she'd moved to the Bay Area. It held a bit of nostalgia for her, as if she were going home, even though her actual home and family were back in Ohio.

Her little sister Chloe had been accepted into the nursing program at Stanford University, which was a big deal. She was following in Raine's footsteps by attending Stanford, and she'd also have some family here, something Raine didn't have.

Heading back to her alma mater brought a lot of other feelings back as well.

Marcus did a double take at her from behind the steering wheel.

"What?" he said. "What's going on inside that mind of yours?"

She smiled. "Nothing."

"Why do people always say that?"

She shrugged. It was true. It wasn't the fact that nobody ever had 'nothing' going on inside his or her mind; it was a matter of filtering what you thought others wouldn't care to hear. When someone asks how you're doing, they weren't asking because they wanted to know. That's just how it worked.

She had intended take the trip by herself, but thought it'd be a great idea to invite Marcus along. She'd been excluding him lately. The last thing she wanted to do was to shut him out when she needed him the most. It wasn't fair to invite him into her life if she was only planning to keep him right at the edge of her inner self.

"How was it, getting back into the swing of things?" Marcus checked his mirrors before merging into the next lane.

"It was great. Anything for normalcy, you know. I enjoy working with the detective, especially if I can help them, but it's nice to have my own gig back. Plus, that couple reminded me that it's time to hire another psychologist."

"Hence this trip," he concluded.

She nodded. As she watched the trees outside the car blur by, she shifted in her seat. They were alone in the car. It was the perfect moment, if any. "Marcus... there are some things I haven't been telling you, and I feel guilty about it."

"I know."

How could he possibly know? Had he tracked her phone? Did someone else tell? Does he think he knows but he doesn't actually have any idea what she's talking about?

"I know when you aren't yourself, Raine. At first it was hard to differentiate between what was part of your healing process, and what was new. I know they haven't found that guy yet, and I know you. I wouldn't doubt you've already begun to try tracking him down."

She had to keep her mouth from dropping open. He was right. And he wasn't pissed, like she thought he would be. She'd underestimated him. "How can you be so supportive and patient with me? Anyone else would have been gone by now."

Marcus pulled over at a spot overlooking a great hill of rolling green off the I-280. "Because none of this was your fault."

Guilt surfaced again for her recent lack of attention. "You're a great guy."

"You're worth it."

All her inhibitions flew out the window. She leaned forward and grabbed his collar, pulling him over for a kiss.

She felt the connection with him all through her whole body.

Nothing else mattered.

Her fears of intimacy melted. She'd been so distant, and so emotionally unavailable to him, the person she was closest to. She wasn't sure how it would feel or what it would bring up if and when she reconnected with Marcus.

But the truth of the matter was that in that moment, he was the only being on Earth that mattered, and it made her whole. He was trust. He was stability.

He wasn't just her old life, there to haunt her. He was her future.

Raine and Marcus decided that splitting up tasks at the college would be the fastest way. They posted the job description and contact information around the Department of Psychology. Marcus was going to go to the head of the department and department chairs to ask about sending some good referrals their way.

Raine was going to go back to the faculty offices and speak directly with the professors from the department, who could recommend or direct graduate students that were close to finishing their degrees. It was weird walking through the hallways again. She hardly remembered her last year of being here. She was constantly sleep deprived and completely buried in her work. It wasn't easy, but she loved every minute of it.

135

She stopped at a staircase. These stairs led to the basement of the psychology building, the very basement that housed the prison experiment that took place back in the 70s. Even as a student here she knew about it, it was a notorious case study that they still researched today in classrooms. But now, the building held far more meaning for her. She'd experienced that case study firsthand on a level that nobody else could understand.

She turned back to the nearest office, one that she'd been quite familiar with when she went to school here. The name on the door was Lilly Everstien. A name she was not familiar with. She'd expected this office to belong to someone else, but perhaps he was no longer here. He was older, and she knew he'd taught psychology at this school for more years than she'd been alive. She felt sadness at the thought that he could have passed away, and she didn't know. Of course, who would tell her anyway?

"Can I help you?" A petite voice squeaked out behind her.

She wheeled around to see a small woman with a polka dotted blouse and cat's eye glasses. "Oh, yes. I was looking for Dr. Jensen? His office used to be here."

"Who's asking?" She was snippy.

"Dr. Raine Walsh, I'm an alumni of his." She spoke with confidence, because if she'd learned anything, it was that speaking with confidence about anything made it seem as though you belonged there without question.

She bit her lip. "He's moved. He's in room 286."

Raine was surprised the woman gave her any information at all. She reached into her bag for her business card, and handed it to the woman. "My partner and I are looking to fill a position in our clinical practice. We have a spot open for a new psychologist. As alumni of this department, we wanted to start here. If you know of anybody interested, please send them my way." She smiled, trying to break through this woman's shell.

Lilly nodded. "286 is that way." She pointed and turned away.

Embarrassed, Raine gathered herself and left, heading into the stairwell.

What was that all about? she asked herself as she climbed the stairs. The woman acted like she owned the place. Did she recognize Raine? She seemed younger. She definitely made her feel like she didn't belong here. *Weird.*

When she reached room 286, she saw him before he saw her.

"Professor Jensen," she called.

Without looking, he waved her into the office.

She walked in and left the door open behind her, taking a seat at the desk covered with towers of books. His office was small, with books stacked everywhere, and completely and utterly disorganized. She felt claustrophobic, wanting to rearrange, dust off, and at least straighten the books and journals.

"You know, they have the internet now." She made the joke, unsure if he'd even find it funny.

"I didn't think I'd ever see you again." His voice was soft.

She remembered sitting in his classroom and listening to his lectures back in the day. He was a good storyteller. A good manipulator. She'd hang on his every word and then he'd crush the lecture at the end. He was a good mentor when she wrote her dissertation. But he was a little strange. She just chalked it up to 'what psychology professor wasn't a little strange?' That was demonstrated nicely by Professor Lilly Everstien from downstairs.

She wasn't sure how to take his statement, so she went with her gut. "Do I not seem like the kind of student to pay visits to her old professors?" she asked.

He swiveled the chair around and peered at her through his round glasses. It was funny that he looked so much Sigmund Freud. He had a trimmed white beard and was bald on the center of his head. The crease between his eyebrows always made him look like he was either angry, or thinking deeply about something.

"No, not that."

Her mind immediately floated to her next thought, that she could have been murdered. Maybe that's what he meant by he never thought he'd see her again. She tried to recall what had been said by the media. She was kidnapped and announced dead. Her family mourned her. And then she was found alive in a landfill. Nobody knew anything other than that. *Did Jensen?* "Oh, well I'm here."

"I see that." He shuffled into his papers on the desk. How he found *anything* in this office was a mystery. He was smart and a tad scatterbrained when she had him as a professor, now he just appeared to be falling apart.

"Professor, I'm here to ask for your help. I'm running a clinical psychology practice with Marcus Altor. We're trying to fill a position, and I was hoping you could post our fliers and talk about it in your classes, if you didn't already have a student in mind."

"Shut the door."

She tipped her head with curiosity. She preferred to keep the door open for obvious reasons. She felt vulnerable closing the door and being alone with him. Of course she would never admit that.

He didn't turn to look at her, and she worried that he would sense her hesitation. Her mind also wondered what he could possibly want to tell her that he couldn't say with the door open. That was enough for her to oblige him. She glanced up and down the hallway and closed the door.

When it clicked, he spoke again. "You're asking a favor of me, when you wouldn't even consider my question years ago?" His voice was low. Deep.

It caught her off guard, but she knew exactly what he was talking about. "I didn't realize it meant that much to you. I just couldn't commit. Is it still going strong?"

"We've lost a few members. But that just means there's another spot open." He raised his eyebrow.

He was talking about a club for psychology alumni. An invitation was an honor, and if she remembered correctly, the membership was completely secret. Rumor had it, it was somewhat of a cult. She declined her invitation, mostly because of the time commitment, in spite of her curiosity.

"After all this time, you're asking me again?" She crossed her arms over her chest.

"Members are chosen carefully. There are strict requirements."

"Can I ask what those are?"

"No."

"I'd like to know how I qualify." She was getting frustrated. This conversation was beginning to irritate her. Where was Marcus? Was he getting further in their search than she was? She wasn't expecting this, especially since she'd forgotten it was even a thing to begin with. Clearly it meant a lot to him. "And after all this time."

"If anything, you are more qualified now."

Was he referring to her nightmare? "How could you possibly know that if we haven't been in contact, Dr. Jensen?" She narrowed her eyes.

"Allen Brink was a student of mine."

Her throat began to constrict. She'd never heard his last name before, but she knew exactly which Allen he was referring to. A range of emotions played in her eyes and she said, "If you have any information regarding the whereabouts of that man, you need to come forward now. I sure as hell hope that you're not trying to say that you knew he was going to do what he did."

"All I said was that he was a student of mine. You of all people should know that assumptions can be made of certain people."

She couldn't help but think that he was downplaying what he knew after he saw her reaction.

"All I ask is that you reconsider." His voice went from solemn, to happy, upbeat, and nonchalant.

"And all I ask is that you post our job description around the building, and let me know if you have a referral." She brought the conversation back full circle.

He nodded, the same curve of skinny lips plain inside the trimmed white beard. "Send me the file and I'll get it posted, Doctor Raine Walsh."

She twisted the doorknob. But before she left, she turned back. "Professor?" she asked softly.

"Hm?"

"Are you familiar with a man named Vinnie Wilson?"

He stopped shuffling. "Sounds familiar. Might have been a student of mine, a while back though. Why do you ask?"

"He's the reason I'm here." She played into his interest in the mysterious side of things, to see if she could get anything more from him.

He hesitated. "I thought you said you were here to recruit?"

"Vinnie is one of my clients so I can't say much. But he told me he was Stanford alum. That reminded me that my alma mater was a good place to start."

"Aye. Well I hope you find what you're looking for." He swiveled around as if he wanted to declare that he was done with this conversation.

"As do I," she replied, and slammed the door behind her. She hurried away, pulling her phone out of her pocket to see where she could catch up with Marcus.

What the hell just happened? she asked herself as she took the stairs two at a time. Her mind was struggling to understand the exchange she'd just had. She had no idea that the exclusive club she'd been invited to back in her senior year was so important to him, and that her declining involvement in it was something he did not take lightly.

What did he know about the Warden? Did he know anything? This anger that someone, especially someone she had been close to as a mentor, would keep information like that a secret. And for what? To protect Allen? What allegiance did Jensen have to the Warden? And was there a connection to Vinnie? Sure, Vinnie was a weird guy, but did he actually have a relationship with the professor? There was no way she'd be able to find out, since sessions were confidential. Maybe they could have a conversation about the school in general, and maybe where he'd spent his time.

Maybe he knew or had information about this exclusive club—maybe he knew nothing about it at all.

TWENTY

Vinnie

innie waited in a parking lot until he saw the pesky
detective's car disappear down the road. He already
called the DMV to let them know he was going to
be late today. Said he needed to take the baby to a doctor's
appointment. They didn't care enough to check into it. His
mind was in and out of blurred confusion, more when he
thought about the next kill.

He put pressure on his eyes. The twitch subsided, until
he let go. Vinnie scrambled out of the car, heading in the
direction of Jonah's apartment.

He took the wooden stairs, one after another, like a
metronome. When he reached the door, he tried the knob.
Locked. No doubt Jonah's doing. The partner rarely locked it.

He pulled a pin from his pocket and knelt down. He
shoved the pin into the key slot, twisting and poking at the
mechanism inside until he felt the lever.

With a quiet *click*, it unlocked.

He opened the door a crack and looked inside. The
coast was clear.

Vinnie slipped into the apartment and secured the door.

Apart from a hissing air vent, the only noise in the apartment came from the bathroom. A running faucet. Someone was here, just as he expected.

He crept towards the bathroom, careful of every noise, every step. The closer he got to the sound of running water, the faster his heart beat.

He turned the hall corner, and stopped in his tracks. The door was open. He could see the man's reflection in the foggy bathroom mirror. He was applying deodorant, a forest green towel wrapped around his hips.

When the man showed no sign of seeing Vinnie in the mirror, he continued towards him, step by step.

As he neared, he heard the man humming to himself. Vinnie was close enough to touch him, and he wrapped his arms around the man in front of the bathroom mirror.

Benjamin yelped, then leaned back into Vinnie. "I thought you'd already left for work, Jo—"

"He did."

Benjamin struggled out of the embrace and backed up against the vanity, staring at Vinnie's face. "Oh! It's you. You scared me." He smiled with his straight, white teeth.

Vinnie stifled a laugh. "Are you disappointed?" He pouted and furrowed his brow, then reached out to grab Ben's hands. "I couldn't stay away."

Benjamin's cheeks grew rosy as he tilted his chiseled chin at Vinnie. "You shouldn't have come here, Kyle. Jonah and I are in a good place now. I'm done messing around."

Benjamin calling him Kyle confirmed that his plan thus far had worked. He could be anyone he wanted to be. And this idiot believed him. Vinnie felt a pang of annoyance. He was losing Benjamin. He needed to get him back. "You don't want me anymore?" he coaxed. It was a slippery slope of lies. He knew that. But if he wanted to destroy the detective that was on to him, he needed to start with his heart.

"No, it's not that. Look. I had a great time with you at the club, don't get me wrong, it's just... Well, I think I love Jonah."

Bingo. The heart. "He doesn't... appreciate you like I do." Vinnie ran his hands down Benjamin's chest, his non-bandaged hand lingering on Ben's hipbone, just above the towel.

He watched Benjamin close his eyes. He slipped his hand under the towel.

"No. Kyle. I told you I can't anymore, okay?"

Vinnie pulled his hand away and backed up. He could go to the kitchen and grab a blade right now. Why was he beating around the bush? Why was he making this more complicated than it needed to be? That was far less humiliating than this current circumstance. He could end it.

But it wasn't part of the plan.

It wasn't the routine. And when he didn't follow routine, he made mistakes. That was clear from the man he'd thought he killed on the side of the interstate. That was a huge mistake, and it exposed his every vulnerability.

His hands began to tremble, and he backed out of the bathroom. "I'm sorry. I shouldn't have come here," he whispered, wide-eyed.

"No- Kyle, it's just—"

Benjamin's voice was muffled, far away at the end of a tunnel, as he turned on his heel and stumbled from the bathroom, through the apartment, and out the door. He didn't look back.

He jumped into his car. Before he started the ignition, he took a cup from the center console and pried off the lid. He threw the water into his face. He needed to cleanse himself of his actions. He was willing to go the extra mile, posing as a homo, just to get what he wanted.

He shook his head, the water on his face sprayed in all directions.

Who am I? What have I become?

"How do you feel about being here?"

He shifted on the couch, and replied with a shrug. He smoothed his hair back over his ears. "It makes my wife happy," he mumbled and looked up at the young psychologist. How they ended up with Raine Walsh was beside him. *Shouldn't she be in therapy herself?* He didn't think she was even practicing again after her *ordeal*.

"Does it make *you* happy?"

"I don't really see the point." He watched her body language. She was insecure, and they were on her territory. He fed off that, using it to sink further and further into his own mind. Deep in the confines of his mind was a safe place. It was the place he ran to at the Christmas party, so long ago. When the memory of the cackling laughter and humiliation came over him, he hunkered down inside himself and found that place of contentment.

There were cracks inside this sanctuary.

And the urge pushed at him from inside.

The urge.

The familiar feeling. He was beginning to lose sight of his goal. He'd been planning this one for weeks. He had already chosen the new license plates. The Detective and his personal life were a distraction. And it almost got him. But he was centered on what mattered now.

A voice at the end of the tunnel.

"Vinnie, try to focus here." Her voice pierced through his dark cloud.

He blinked and saw the therapist sitting across from him. Her couch was itchy through his pants. The flowery scent in the room made him resent his wife.

"What do you want from me?"

"We're just chatting here. You don't have to give me anything. We can sit here the whole session if you'd like.

Your wife has her own agenda, but that's separate from what goes on here. We can spend this time however you'd like."

He pretended to be thinking about her words.

The man would be at that football game. A professional football game, with lots of people there. It was the perfect setup, almost too easy. And he had an alibi. The game itself. It was a great cover.

"You seem to have a lot on your mind."

"Gwen," he whispered.

"Tell me about Gwen."

He tried to pull out of his thoughts. "I could be a better husband."

"How?"

"Pay more attention to her. Appreciate what she does for the baby."

"I know she would like that."

Yeah, I bet she would. His thoughts flickered on visualizing the parking lot, the tailgaters, the reflector vest traffic and parking attendants...

That detective guy, Jonah. He came to the DMV. He'd been watching his house. Long before he came to the door, he'd definitely known something was up. But he didn't have any proof. *How could he?*

I clean up well.

"Do you like to write, Vinnie?"

He shook his thoughts away. "Huh?"

"I asked if you like to write."

"Why?" A pounding headache emerged from his temporal lobe.

"You need to express your thoughts. I'd suggest you try and get them out on a page. Just sitting here, I can tell you're burdened. You don't have to live with that, Vinnie."

For a moment, for one small, fleeting moment he actually believed her. Maybe she *could* help him? Maybe she could take all the pain away, all this darkness.

Maybe the darkness was deeper than a Christmas party. Maybe it came from something buried deep. A childhood that ended prematurely.

Screw this.

Therapy? Why was he even here? He didn't need therapy. Gwen needed therapy. Gwen was suffering from postpartum depression. And she was bringing him into this. He was wasting his time, and Raine Walsh was wasting hers.

"Sure, I'll write," he mumbled. He saw her smile and scratched the back of his head.

I've got to get out. I've got to get out.

He stood. "Gwen can book the next appointment." He nodded at her and started for the door.

"We still have the rest of the hour, Vinnie. You're welcome to stay."

"Naw, thanks though." He could hardly even hear himself mutter those last few words as he sunk deeper. He had work to do. And all his energy was devoted to that. He wanted to feel well again. He'd forgotten what it felt like to have relief. It was time.

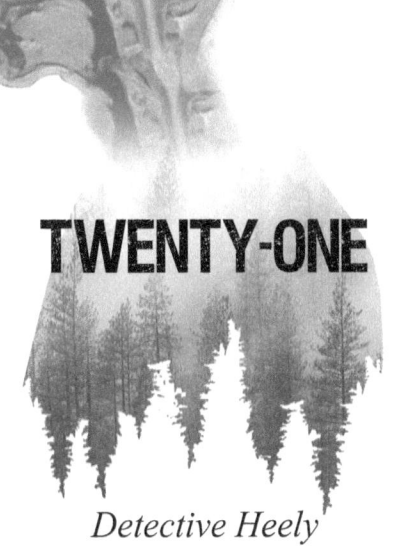

TWENTY-ONE

Detective Heely

Good! *I'm glad he knows I'm watching. I'm going to push him harder,* Jonah thought to himself as he parked his car. He sat there a moment before cutting the ignition and hopping out. This was a slow street with few, if any cars passing by. It would be a safe place to leave his car for the time being. He hoofed into the neighborhood. He was aware of his surroundings, noticing every detail along the way. Who was outside on their lawn, grabbing the mail, walking their dog, kids getting off the bus. There wasn't much movement, but he also looked at all the houses for open curtains. He couldn't be seen. He needed to be smart.

When he was sure that nobody was around, he pushed into a hedge and turned around, butted up against one of Vinnie's neighbor's shed. From here, he could see into the one car garage. The dandelions were taller than the grass, spreading across the small neglected front yard.

Nobody would see him here. He could camp out until Vinnie came home, and he would be able to see if he went anywhere after that. He thought about going up to the house and asking the wife some questions, but he decided against it. First off, if she was even home, she could already know about what her husband was. But it was very likely that she didn't know anything. He'd seen that happen many times. He could pose as someone else, but it was also possible that she'd seen him there before, and that would also warn them. Then there was the chance that Vinnie could come home from work and catch him. And then the cat was out of the bag.

It was safer to sit back and wait.

But it wasn't comfortable. He wanted to be at the ready, so he was kneeling down to the ground but balancing on his toes. A branch was jabbing his ribcage, and he tried to move away, but another took its place. There were also no doubt some creepy crawling things ready to go up his back.

He reached to the small of his back to check his gun. Even as an undercover, he was always armed.

It crossed his mind that he wasn't even entirely sure what he was waiting for, except he knew the guy would screw up sooner or later, and he wanted and needed to be there to see it happen. If this really was his guy, then he'd already screwed up once.

Shit, Kevin! He could have very easily shown Kevin a photo of Vinnie to see if Kevin could identify him. Of course, he did say it was dark and he wasn't necessarily coherent, but the possibility was still there. He just felt like sometimes the minutia held him back. The paperwork slowed him down and he had something to prove. To himself. To his team back at the office. He had to prove that he was worthy. He never wanted to be a patrol officer again. Doing the same old thing every day. Pissing people off by writing them a ticket when they're already late for work. He couldn't imagine himself back there. Not to mention he'd already put his all into this case. He'd spent so much time away from family and friends, away from Benjamin, dedicating his life and all his time to this.

And his father, who'd had a successful career as a detective and expected nothing but accuracy from him.

He. Could. Not. Fail.

He was starting to sway on his feet, when a car finally pulled into the driveway.

It was him.

The car stopped halfway up the driveway.

Jonah's held his breath as if Vinnie could hear it.

But then the car continued into the garage.

It didn't shut behind him. Vinnie rounded the vehicle, unbuttoning the top buttons of his shirt as he looked around once, then disappeared into the house.

Jonah exhaled, holding onto his chest. He strained to see into the garage. Vinnie left the door open, and it was a good opportunity to see if there was anything of interest inside. As much as he could see from his spot inside the hedge.

Jonah made sure to keep an eye on the rest of the neighborhood as well, so he wasn't seen peeking on them from the bushes.

While he trained his eyes on the vehicle, trying to catch the license plate number to run it against with the tow driver's records, his phone rang and vibrated from inside his pants pocket. He flinched. He should have put it on silent, and he was grateful it hadn't gone off while Vinnie was in earshot. The feeling was equal to the rush of adrenaline and embarrassment you get when your phone goes off in court or church, somewhere you should have turned your phone off beforehand, and were even told to, but forgot.

He wrestled the phone from his pocket and clicked the button that silenced the ring. He looked down at the caller ID and clicked the answer button.

Raine Walsh.

"Yeah? Now's not a good time," he whispered into the smartphone.

"Heely, this is important."

"Can we talk bout this later?" He started to turn it off, but she spoke.

"No."

"What the hell?"

"I've waited long enough. You keep putting me off."

"What's this about?" he asked.

"It's about the ME report I saw on your desk."

"When you were snooping?"

"That's beside the point. You made a deal with me."

Jonah looked around and tucked himself closer the shed. He needed to pay attention. He thought about hanging up, but he did owe her some explanation. "Raine. Please. I am hiding outside what is potentially the Bystander Killer's house right now. I will meet with you when I leave and we can talk, okay?"

"Are you serious? Heely! Does anyone know you're there?"

"Now you do." He heard her quietly cursing.

"Where are you?"

"Nice try Raine, but I'm not bringing you into this."

"What's that supposed to mean? I'm already in it."

"Dammit, woman, seriously. This is for your safety."

"I have a feeling you're not following protocol your-self."

Vinnie walked into the garage again.

"He's back," he whispered and ended the call.

Vinnie looked out the garage door and down the drive-way. There was no way he'd heard Jonah, but he was atten-tive.

What surprised him was the oversized, shiny red and gold jersey Vinnie was wearing. He looked completely out of place. His slimy black hair stuck out of the bottom of a baseball cap with the 49ers logo.

Vinnie pulled out of the garage, closed the door, backed down the driveway, then eased his way up the road.

Football jersey? He was headed to the game.

When the car had turned the corner and was out of sight, Jonah checked the house to make sure no window blinds or curtains were open, a wife watching her husband leave. When he was sure, he popped out of the hedge. He speed-walked back to his car. One foot after the other, his body could not move fast enough across the gravel. His shirt felt drenched at his underarms. He was dripping sweat. He looked up at the bridge as he rounded the corner.

There was no car.

He looked up at the street signs to make sure he hadn't come down the wrong road.

He hadn't.

Where was his car?

"Shit!"

He was most surprised because he wasn't expecting it. This did not happen. And he knew exactly who had done it. How did Vinnie get to his car and move it so quickly? How was he always one step ahead?

Then it hit him as he thought through the conversation at the DMV. Vinnie had warned him. He told him flat out, "I know you've been watching. I've been watching you too.

He ripped his phone out of his jeans and pressed the callback button.

She answered right away.

"Listen, I'm going to turn on location services. Track my phone and come get me."

"What's going on?" Raine asked.

"I don't have any time to explain."

"Kay, stay put. I'm there."

He hung up and paced the curb.

It felt like too much time had passed since he hung up with her. He ran through all the details in his mind. He kept feeling for his gun and his phone. He pulled up the stadium on his phone and studied all the entry and exit points. He studied the parking lots and how they were laid out. Chances were if this was Vinnie's plan, he had no intention of actually going to the game, especially when everyone had to pass through a metal detector to get in. Was there a chance he could go through an employee entrance? Naw, he was wearing a jersey when he left, he was posing as a fan.

Her car pulled up and she unlocked the doors. He hopped into the passenger seat. "We need to go to Levi's Stadium."

She nodded and peeled out.

"Were you working out?" he asked, looking at her attire.

She was wearing a red racer back yoga shirt and black pants.

"Shouldn't I be the one asking the questions?" she retorted.

"I'm sorry I involved you. You were just getting your life back on track and—"

"I'm happy to help, Jonah. But you need to keep me in the loop. Calling me in emergency situations? I mean, what are we even going into? What should I expect?"

"I think this guy is going for his next kill at the stadium. He prefers to kill by stabbing. In public places. The construction site, the side of a highway, an apartment building, and now a sporting event. I know it's him. I tracked him down."

"Then why don't you call it in?"

Dumbfounded, he tried to think of a polite response. "I *am* the police."

She laughed. "I mean, why aren't you asking for backup?"

"Well, I went about this in an unconventional way. And I haven't been using state resources the whole time anyway.

I sort of found him on my own. I've broken a lot of rules, but it had to be done."

"Jonah, I want to ask you about that autopsy report. Brandon was important to me. And if what those papers said is true, I'd like to speak with his family. Can I at least do that? You said I should be getting my life back together, right? Can you at least do that for me?"

"Yes. I'll get you the information after we're through with this."

He was still upset that she had snooped, and she didn't know the whole story, but he did owe her the information, and an explanation. It was just hard to concentrate on that right now.

When they pulled into a parking lot at Levi's Stadium, understanding hit him in the face like a bag of sand. Yes, Vinnie had been out of place wearing that jersey. But here, he was one in a sea of thousands wearing the same thing. Here, he belonged. He was one of the crowd. Here was the perfect place to commit a murder where nobody would remember your face, because you look like the guy next to every other guy at the game. And here, there were enough people to put the bystander effect into place.

Would they ever find him?

"Raine, you hang out here and I'll be right back. I need to find him."

"Wait!" she shouted and grabbed his arm.

"What's your plan?"

He crinkled his nose.

"You don't have a plan?"

"It's better if we split up. Divide and conquer. Ping my phone if you see him."

"I don't even know what he looks like! And I don't have a way to defend myself!"

"You're Raine Walsh. You don't have a way to defend yourself?" he asked, actually quite shocked.

She looked down at herself. "I came in a hurry. I might have something in my glove compartment..."

"Here." He knelt down and pulled the pistol from his ankle holster. Then he pulled off his jacket. "Hide it in the waistband of your pants—use the jacket to cover it up."

She nodded.

He started to leave again when he felt her touch his arm.

"Stay safe."

He half smiled. "You too." Then he was out of the car and running into the crowd.

TWENTY-TWO

Raine

Raine watched Heely through the windshield as long as she could before he disappeared into the crowd. She pulled the jacket around her to conceal the gun. She'd tucked it inside the waistband of her pants, up against her hipbone. She kept her eyes peeled. She didn't even know what this Bystander Killer looked like, so she couldn't find him in the crowd even if she wanted to.

She pulled her phone out and kept it close, in case Heely called her. She tapped her foot, feeling antsy. She couldn't stand not knowing what was going on. Being in the dark. Not being able to help. She looked down at her phone. What was she thinking? She should have called for help long ago, when Heely first called her. Of course he was the police. And originally she didn't trust authorities to help her get shit done. From her experience, if she wanted to live, then it had to be by her own will. Nobody was going to climb that tower and rescue her. Trusting authority was difficult.

So it only made sense that when Heely told her he 'had' it, and that he didn't need backup, she didn't trust him either. So what if he was doing things 'off the books.'

She felt conflicted whether to call for help, especially after Jonah told her that he didn't need backup. It was a matter of him getting in trouble for going off the reservation, or his life. She wasn't about to cost any more people their lives. She called.

After she hung up with police, she stood outside the car and leaned against the door. The fresh air felt good.

A shrill scream echoed across the lot.

She took off running in the direction of the scream, pumping one arm and holding the gun against her body with the other. The people were getting thicker and closer together, running in all directions. She didn't hear any gunshots, so she hoped nobody was hurt. Using everything she had, she pushed people out of the way and plunged into the middle of the crowd.

She saw Jonah first. He was on the pavement, curled up. Everything blurred around her, she could only see him on the ground, clutching his side. She fell onto her knees and touched his shoulder.

"Jonah. What happened, what's going on?" She leaned him back and saw the crimson soaking into his tee shirt. Instinctively, she applied pressure, the red garish against her white skin. Jonah's breathing rattled and he bent over, grabbing at her arm.

"Hey!" She used her other hand to slap his cheek. "Stay with me. You hear me? Jonah." She looked up. "Where's stadium security!" she yelled at the crowd of fans in jerseys. The Bystander Effect was in full effect. And then it hit her. He was here. He stabbed Jonah. But the detective wasn't his next victim. And if the killer was here, his next victim was too.

And Jonah already knew this. He was in the thick of it. He pointed in the direction of another body on the ground with people hovering over it. "I'm... I'm okay, I jus' got nicked. Go help him."

"I called for backup after you left. A unit is on the way. As well as stadium security."

"Go help him!" he yelled, clutching his side and wincing.

She pulled her bloodied hand from his ribs and scurried over to the other body, almost tripping over her own feet.

"Back. Back!" She shoved people out of the way to get to him. He looked like any other guy at the game. Jeans and a 49ers jersey. A baseball cap, ordinary frat boy features. The only difference was the pool of blood he was lying in.

Raine was no doctor, but she'd experienced trauma a time or two, and she was the first responder here. She had to see if there was anything they could do. She lifted the jersey and unbuttoned his pants, then pulled them away, all while a woman screamed and cried, tugging on the man and batting at Raine in hysterics. She felt like her limbs were dragging through sand in slow motion. She looked down at the man's wound, a slit from one side to the other, organs protruding. She grabbed his wrist and tried to find a pulse, feeling the woman's weight pulling on her.

"Raine—"

She heard Jonah croaking her name. She dropped the wrist and stumbled back and knelt with him. She heard the faint sound of a siren approaching. "He ran." Jonah grabbed her arm. "Get my wallet. There's a note in there with an address."

He winced as he turned to let her reach his back pocket and get his wallet.

With her bloody hands, she opened it, sifting through the bills to find the address. If she remembered correctly, the address wasn't far from where she had just picked Jonah up. But why did he want her to go to the killer's house? "I don't want to leave you," she insisted, her hands shaking as she looked down at his wound again.

"He has a wife and baby. Go there. Make sure they're safe."

The siren in the background got louder.

"Go! I'll be fine."

She nodded and stood. She pulled off his jacket, folded it, and put it on his ribs. "Hold this tight. Paramedics will be right here, okay?"

He nodded, and she took off running, holding the gun close and trying to conceal it. The crowd was a blur in the background of a horrific event.

TWENTY-THREE

Raine

S he stumbled back to her car, forgotten by the milling crowd. She fumbled with her keys then revved the engine, peeling out before she had a chance to think. She dropped the gun in the passenger seat. She hated guns. She wasn't even entirely sure she knew how to fire it.

It would only take a few minutes to get to the address. She tried to wipe the blood from her hands on her black yoga pants; the deep crimson blended into the dark fabric. She didn't know what she was going into. She didn't think Jonah would knowingly send her into danger, but the situation was unpredictable. And she wanted somebody coherent to know where she was. She felt guilty before for not sharing her whereabouts with her boyfriend when she should have. She grabbed the phone in the center console, pressed her favorites and shakily held it to her ear.

"Hello?"

"Marcus."

"Raine? What's wrong, babe? Where are you?" His tone said he'd caught the urgency in her voice.

"I'm on a case with Detective—" her throat caught, "—Heely. He's sent me to an address to collect the wife and child of our suspected murderer."

"Raine. Where? Give me that address. I'll be right there."

"No! I didn't call to involve you. It's okay. We've already called the police. I'm just freaking out a little."

"Heely wouldn't send you somewhere dangerous..." The line was quiet. "Would he? You're not trained! I mean, sure you're psychologically trained, but if the killer gets there before you—"

"There's a baby, Marcus. A woman and an innocent baby."

"How do you know the wife wasn't involved? A SWAT team should be going in there. Listen, I know you're smart, Raine. Just, please call me when you're safe. I don't know if I can sit here and wait for you. It scares the shit outta me. I don't want to come see you injured in a hospital again, or worse. When you were in that coma, Raine, it destroyed me. Please."

She felt the embrace in his words. She felt like she mattered.

"Marcus, I love you."

"You are strong. I love you too."

She clicked off the line and dropped her phone on the passenger seat with the gun as she turned onto the little suburban street.

This was it.

She parked outside the house and jumped out, then leaned back in for the gun and her phone. She wished for a moment that she'd known all this was going to be going on, because she really wasn't dressed for this. She pushed her phone down into her sports bra, holding it up against her chest, and she held onto the gun down by her leg as she rounded the car and walked up to the house. The garage door was open, but empty.

She thought about going to the front door, but she needed to be quick and there was access through the garage.

She couldn't believe she was doing this alone. Marcus was right. She wasn't a police officer. She wasn't a social worker. She was a psychologist. This was not anything she knew how to cope with. When she agreed to help Heely, she didn't realize it meant fieldwork. And she knew most certainly that he didn't expect this either. But this went beyond assisting Heely with his case. This was her helping other humans. They needed her, and she wanted to do it. Because no one else would get there in time. And time mattered dearly.

She slipped into the garage and heard a screaming baby. She entered the house through the door in the garage.

The man was hovering over a portable playpen in the family room.

Raine raised the gun and held it with both hands. "Stop right there."

He hadn't heard her come in because of the baby screaming.

She lowered the gun. "Vinnie Wilson?" She looked down at herself, covered in blood and back at her client, a man she'd been seeing in her office. It couldn't be. Vinnie Wilson, the Bystander Killer? It must be a mistake. How could he be? How could she not have caught a hint of his tendencies? How could he have hidden that?

"What are you doing here, Dr. Walsh?" he asked, his voice wheezy.

"You—you killed all those people?" she whispered, still unsure it wasn't a dream.

He turned back to the playpen.

"Don't you touch Scarlett." She raised the gun again.

"What? You gonna shoot me?" he asked.

She didn't want to. He was sick. He'd hurt people, but it wasn't him. It wasn't Vinnie. It was the demon he carried around inside him. And she was just beginning to tap into that. There was so much about him that she didn't know, and she wanted to help him. She was reminded of the young man that committed suicide in her office last year. The one whose father came knocking on her door. He was sick too, and she couldn't save him. But Vinnie, he had a wife and a baby.

"Where's Gwen?"

"She wasn't here when I got here," he whispered. "She left the baby right here."

She didn't believe him. Gwen would never leave the baby.

"What did you do to her? Vinnie. Did you stab her too?"

He didn't reply.

Just keep him talking... just keep him talking, she told herself, trying to stall enough for the police to catch up with her. "We can figure this out, okay? Why don't you take a seat on the ground there, okay?" She tried to coax him, taking a step forward.

His eyes shifted and she stopped again.

"I can't help it," he hissed.

"You can't help what? Sitting?"

"I can't help..." He shifted and a metal object caught the light, and flickered at her eye. It was a knife. A long knife.

"Vinnie, you don't have to do this." She didn't want to have to hurt him. But if he posed a threat, she would have to. It also occurred to her that she didn't even really know how to fire a gun. Of course, she'd been taught how in the self-defense classes she'd taken in the past, but this was real life. And the weight of the gun in her hands reminded her that she'd never pointed one at a human before.

And then it all happened rapidly.

She saw him lunge at her. Caught off guard, she stum-bled back into the wall, hitting her head before she slipped to the ground, her chin slamming into her chest. She didn't drop the gun.

Vinnie raised the knife, and then he stopped. Frozen, eyes wide and a look of surprise on his face.

Raine couldn't understand what was happening at first, but then she saw her. A woman stood behind him, and Vinnie fell over on his side, clutching his stomach. His wife stood there holding a kitchen knife.

She stepped over Vinnie.

Raine felt her head pounding where she'd hit the wall. Gwen dropped the knife and turned to pick up her still screaming baby.

Police flooded the house through the front door and the garage.

"Medic!"

"Weapon!"

"All clear!" Words from everywhere. Raine huddled with Gwen and Scarlett.

"Dr. Walsh?" A woman police officer asked, then reached down and retrieved the gun that she was still holding.

"It's Jonah Heely's," she explained.

"I know. Come with me, we need to get you to a medic."

"It's not my blood. Take care of Gwen and Scarlett." She looked back to try and catch a glimpse of Vinnie. She had no idea what kind of wound Gwen was forced to inflict on him. But there were so many people in the house, she couldn't even tell if he was still on the floor or not.

"Someone else will assist them, Doctor. Come with me."

Raine reached out with her bloodstained hand and took Gwen's hand, it too covered in blood, the blood of the killer. "Thank you."

Gwen began to sob as they whisked Raine out of the house toward an ambulance.

"Please don't waste your resources on me. I'm okay. How's Jonah?" she asked.

"He's gone to General Hospital East."

"And the other—"

"Didn't make it."

Raine was seated on the back of the ambulance. The paramedic began to poke and pull at her, shining a light in her eyes, and wrapping a blood pressure cuff around her arm.

The case was over. They found the murderer. She was able to help in more ways than she could have imagined. Looking down at her hands as a medic used a wipe to clean them up, she mumbled, "Not my blood."

The sight of the blood was something she felt numb to. Immune. She sat on the back of the ambulance, with the medic probing at the back of her skull. She stared straight ahead. *If I continue to help the police, this will not be the last time I see blood.*

The case she agreed to help on was closed.

Her case was not.

TWENTY-FOUR

Raine

"Hello?" Raine peeked into the hospital room. The smell of the antiseptic reminded her of the week of her life that she'd lost while in a coma. It was this hospital.

"Hey." Jonah nodded at her.

She entered the dimly lit room and sat next to his bed. She pulled out her phone and pretended to hold a pen, using the phone as her notepad. "You've been through a lot and I just need to ask you some questions." She laughed.

The joke was worth it. Jonah actually showed teeth when he smiled, before he winced. "You don't have to tell me I've been through a lot."

She smiled. "Hmm, you're not making much sense, Detective Heely."

He laughed, "I get it, I get it! The shoe is on the other foot."

"Seriously though, how're you feeling?"

"I'm fine. Ready to get outta here. Can't stand being penned up, I've got shit to do."

"He got you pretty good. You're lucky."

"Hey, listen..." He grabbed her hand.

She looked down at it, but allowed him to continue.

"I never should have sent you to that house. I'm sorry for that."

"I know. It's okay. It happened the way it was supposed to."

"I never wanted you to actually be at a scene. You were just supposed to help in the office. And I certainly didn't want to put you into such a traumatic situation."

She wasn't sure whether she should tell him that the Wilsons were her clients. She didn't get much time with them before everything happened. She wondered if she would have gotten the chance to experience Vinnie's darkness. Or any sort of clue to his motivations. "Trauma sort of finds me, I guess." She accepted this fact, which was a big step from where she was a year ago. She accepted that things were sometimes out of her control, and she was learning to become more fluid, so it didn't destroy her.

"You know, Raine? You were a great partner in crime. I'd love it if you'd continue to work with me. You were an invaluable asset. Most of the time I run solo, and I feel like with your help we were able to cover more ground."

Raine sat back in the chair.

"Of course you don't have to make a decision immediately, but..."

"I'm not sure. I feel like I can't fully give myself to the work and helping others, when I don't have closure on my own case."

He nodded. "That's understandable. Listen, I haven't gotten the chance to catch up with you on some of the things going on with the Prison Experiment case."

"The Prison Experiment?" she asked, hearing it for the first time.

"That's what the station has been calling it, I'm sorry if that offends you."

"No, I like it." It tied right back to her background in psychology, making perfect sense because of the Warden's infatuation with the Stanford Prison Experiment. She wondered in that moment if Allen had gone to the same university she had, and the thought sent chills down her spine. The same school she went to. The same school that Vinnie Wilson went to. There couldn't be a connection. It was a big coincidence. Or was it?

She went back to thinking about what he originally said. That he needed to 'catch her up' on details of the case. Did he have any new developments? Was he holding back even more information?

"I've been sort of keeping this from you, because we weren't sure what we found."

She wasn't sure how to digest the information that he was telling her, or if she was even ready. She let him continue.

"When we conducted our search of every potential facility in vicinity—specifically ones with dumpsters from companies that use that landfill—we found one that had been completely gutted, as you'd suggested. Someone moved everything out of there, stripped it down to the studs. Except for one thing. A body."

Raine tensed.

"You knew this already?"

"Uh... When the case wasn't moving quick enough, Arie and I took it upon ourselves to go see what was left, and we saw the stain on the floor."

"How did you find the building?"

"I got the address from one of the reports on your desk. When you took that phone call and left me in there. The body was Brandon Perez's."

"You shouldn't have done that."

"You already knew I did that."

He nodded. "We're past that. Whenever I can get out of here, I'd like you to ID him. Can you do that for me?" he asked.

She thought about it a moment. Brandon meant a lot to her, and was ultimately the one who helped her survive the prison. She felt a connection with him different than her relationship with Arie. But she felt like she owed it to his family. She needed to find closure for everyone. She wanted to speak to his wife and daughter and tell them he was a hero, and she was alive today because of him.

She nodded at Heely. "Okay, I'll go."

The door opened. A guy with broad shoulders and a kind face walked in.

"They didn't have the coffee you wanted, so I just got black—Oh hello?"

Raine hopped out of her seat. "I was just leaving."

"Raine, this is my boyfriend, Benjamin."

Raine reached out and shook his hand. "Nice to meet you. I've been working with Jonah on this case."

Benjamin said, "I've heard a lot about you." His eyes were sympathetic.

She nodded. She wished she could say the same, but what she knew, he probably didn't want to hear. Jonah kept most of his personal life private anyway. She didn't even realize he was gay until he told her, although that was none of her concern.

"I'll catch up with you in a little bit to schedule that appointment. Soon yeah?" she asked Jonah.

He nodded.

"It was nice to meet you, Ben."

"Likewise."

Raine left and headed back to the waiting room. A physician had examined her when the ambulance brought her to the hospital. They released her quickly. She was lucky to have escaped a concussion. She was able to clean up a little, but she couldn't wait to get home to take a shower and wash this case off. When she arrived at the waiting room, the two most important people in her life were there, sitting next to each other.

Arie stood first, throwing his arms around her neck. She embraced him, closing her eyes and smiling. She was happy he was safe, and he looked good. She opened her eyes and saw Marcus watching her with a little smile. He let her enjoy her moment with Arie. Then she turned to Marcus and jumped into his arms. He sniffled next to her ear. *Is he crying?* She rubbed his back, and then backed up to get a good look at his face.

"I'm just happy you're okay. That phone call, man... that was scary."

She was trying to choke back tears herself. "I'm okay."

"You are one incredible woman," he told her.

The noise and commotion of the hospital waiting room faded. She closed her eyes and said, "Lets just go home, yeah?"

She stood back with her arms crossed over her chest as the medical examiner unlocked the freezer drawer. She glanced at Jonah briefly. Then the body slid out of the drawer, draped in a sheet. It felt like something out of a movie. A movie she did not want to star in.

Over the last few days, she tried to prepare herself for this moment. The moment she'd get to see Brandon, even though it wasn't what she wanted to see.

"Are you ready?" asked the attendant.

She nodded.

He peeled back the sheet, and she stumbled into Jonah. He grabbed her by the shoulders to keep her from falling and she leaned on his chest, her hand over her mouth. She stared the body, shaking.

"It's..."

"Is it him?" Jonah asked gently. "We just need a positive ID."

"It's not Brandon."

All the memories of the face in front of her slashed at her psyche. She couldn't breathe. She couldn't stand. She couldn't.

"It's not—Who is it then?" he asked.

"That... is the Warden."

She was in shock, she hardly remembered the attendant covering him back up and pushing his body back into the freezer. She hardly remembered being ushered back into the hall. And she hardly heard the words that Jonah said to her.

"The girl we have locked up for conspiring with him, the crazy thing is... Raine, this morning we got a confession."

Raine didn't understand.

"She confessed to murder. Only we thought this whole time that she'd murdered Brandon Perez. You're telling me, that if that body in there is Allen—this Warden guy, then Megan confessed to murdering her captor... your captor?"

She couldn't believe what she was hearing, but there was also a part of her that did believe it. The red haired girl spent months in jail, unwilling to speak. She'd said things that made Raine believe she thought that Allen would come for her, save her. Raine was so certain of the Stockholm Syndrome theory that she failed to notice that Megan had her own agenda the whole time.

"Megan, although terrible in her own right, also needed closure. And that's exactly what she got."

THE END

WANT TO KNOW WHAT HAPPENS NEXT?

Like this story, each book in the series digs up a psychological experiment from within the archives of our history.
Do people ever tell you that you look familiar, when you've
never met them? Ever wonder if there is another person out
there that looks exactly like you, with no relation? What if
it was on purpose…

If you liked *The Altruism Effect* and *The Bystander Effect*,
you will love the 3rd book in the series:

THE
CARBON
EFFECT

Follow this link for more:
http://kristinhelling.com/CarbonEffect
Thank you for reading!

ABOUT THE AUTHOR

Kristin Helling enjoys stories with a journey- whether it's a journey across the globe, a journey through space, or a journey of finding one's self.

Kristin studied her Bachelors degree in English writing at Park University, and received an 18-hour minor in Psychology. Her favorite classes were *Positive Psych* and *Social Influence and Persuasion.* It was only a matter of time before this passion found its way into her fiction.

She is married to a photographer, and lives outside of Kansas City, Missouri with their two hairy children: a Husky who is terrified of vacuum cleaners, and a Collie-Shepherd mix with more energy than the sun.

www.ingramcontent.com/pod-product-compliance
Lightning Source LLC
Chambersburg PA
CBHW020019030726
47499CB00007B/2183